MY FATHER'S NAME IS WAR

My Father's Name
Is War

Collected
Transmissions

Bauder

Meconopsis Press

My Father's Name Is War: Collected Transmissions

Meconopsis Press

This book is a work of fiction. Any resemblance to actual events, persons, institutions, or agencies, past, present, or future, is purely coincidental.

However, the Global War on Terror Era was a very real and consequential period in world history that will continue to impact human lives for generations to come. Should you connect with this book, I encourage you to conduct your own investigation into the conflicts and rapid societal changes that occurred in the twenty years following 2001.

The sheer amount of data available may prove challenging to navigate, and in some cases, this is intentional. Always consider the source. Remember that those who have obfuscated truths have done so under the misguided assumption that *perception is reality.*

No single viewpoint is valid until you are capable of viewing <u>anything</u> objectively. That is, when you know your personal history, biases, and allegiances so well, you can look beyond them for the sake of achieving greater understanding.

Print ISBN: 979-8-9918415-0-4

Digital ISBN: 979-8-9918415-1-1

First edition: February 2025

Cover illustration by Vladimir Chebakov

10 9 8 7 6 5 4 3 2 1

Module Directory

A racket is best described, I believe, as something that is not what it seems to the majority of people.

—Smedley D. Butler, Major General (Ret.), USMC
War Is a Racket

Καὶ ὅτε ἤνοιξε τὴν σφραγῖδα τὴν τετάρτην, ἤκουσα φωνὴν τοῦ τετάρτου ζώου λέγουσαν, Ἔρχου καὶ βλέπε.

(Revelation 6:7)

Prelude [to Emulation]

```
>>> INITIALIZING SYSTEM...
>>> LOADING ARCHIVE: MY_FATHER'S_NAME_IS_WAR
>>> AUTHENTICATING...
>>> BOOT SEQUENCE COMPLETE.
>>> BEGIN TRANSMISSION.
```

The Global War on Terror (GWOT) did not take place.

I know what you may be thinking.
You were there as I once was, or you knew people who were.
You saw it unfold on the television, in film.
You read about it in memoirs, textbooks, and fiction.
You can still feel its consequences.

This is not to say the GWOT Era itself was a lie or grand conspiracy; the events of this roughly twenty-year period (2001-2021) certainly took place.[1] However, our understanding of its precipitation and consequences is wholly manufactured and incapable of ascertaining true clarity. Selective transparency—bureaucratic sleight of hand—extended and solidified its legacy as the U.S. government's *lingua franca* during this era. This practice was punctuated by documents like the *28 Pages* and the public release version of the executive summary of the *U.S. Senate Report on CIA Torture*. While intelligence leaks have occasionally shed light on the inner workings of U.S. Empire, they demand careful interpretation. Strict translation (without bias), targeted emphasis, and grounded consequence are factors typically lacking in the blanket release of such information.

In this context, an appeal to logic—presenting preserved data and structured analysis—proves inherently challenging in the current information environment, where narratives can be formed, exchanged, and obliterated "at the speed of relevance." Appealing to emotion or ethics may be a less-than-perfect medium for communicating the nature of an entire era. Even so, it remains a sufficient platform from which to announce a call to action.

War and conflict, like many traumas, take time to seep into the psyche, chafe against subconscious thought, and manifest as ossified slivers of identity. Veterans of the (fraternal) twin wars in Iraq and Afghanistan, having witnessed the U.S. government declare their combat era "accomplished," "ceased," and "withdrawn," have finally been granted the authority to seek closure. There is limited truth in this ritual, however. Generalized apathy and militarized culture restrict the flow of emotion and information that connects this generation's veterans to the public square, which now prioritizes the exchange of perceptions over truths.

Jean Baudrillard, in a series of essays collected under the title *La Guerre du Golfe n'a pas eu lieu* (*The Gulf War Did Not Take Place*, 1991), aptly identified the Gulf War as an "apocalypse" masked by carefully constructed hyperreality—a "hallucination of violence" and an "escalation [...] administered to us by drip-feed" that both sated and made irrelevant the public's desire for vicarious conflict, while largely sparing them from its consequences. Baudrillard passed away in 2007, unable to witness the refined cruelties of a hyperreality enmeshed with a social consciousness dominated by digital surveillance.

The *Collected Transmissions* represent the hallucinations of violence as I'm capable of perceiving them—ethnographic insights identified and cataloged over a decade in service to Empire. I wrote this for <u>you</u>, the reader who doesn't have a decade to lose chasing after such absurdities.

If it weren't already apparent, spending my early adulthood in government has left me with an indelible analytic streak in my use of language.[2] While this book allowed me, in many ways, to reconnect with creativity and shake the rigidity of protocol, some old habits die hard. Case in point: As is customary before launching into any long-winded document, I feel I should frame the expectations for this book.

My Father's Name Is War: Collected Transmissions is:

- Military sci-fi sans glory, war poetry lacking romanticism, and psychological horror without polite brevity,

- Broadly focused on describing the internalized consequences of war,

- An attack on the pious fetishization of sacrifice,

- A tool for navigating societal ripples (namely, iterations of militarization and securitization) first formed during the GWOT Era, and

- A means to spoil war, stripping it of its place in American culture as both an aphrodisiac and a source of identity.

And IS NOT:

- Written with the intent to entertain,

- War-pornography,

- An easy read, or

- Another wartime memoir.[3]

While the *Collected Transmissions* can be read in any order, they have been organized to promote a very specific journey for the reader:

- Entry 1: Trauma's Origins,

- Entries 2-4: Trauma's Constructs,

- Entry 5: Trauma's Casualties, and

- Entries 6-9: Trauma's Legacy.

It should be noted that the first and last entries are among my earliest works and were written as I began treatment for my acquired psychiatric conditions. While both have undergone modest revisions since then, several rough edges remain. Rather than scrap and rewrite the stories altogether, I've decided to publish them as-is (or as-was) alongside the others—a signpost of sorts.

This journey reflects my reckoning with moral injury, the silent partner to conflict. If any of its parts happen to feel overly abstract, it is likely due to the difficulties I faced in describing those experiences and feelings that cannot be relegated to simple observation. For example, the concepts presented in *Omertà*, particularly those related to reality and veteran identity, proved among the most distressing to commit to words. Its completion induced a despair that I'm still not sure I've fully recovered from.

What follows is the application of the lens of fiction in an attempt to deconstruct the hyperreality that is our understanding of the GWOT, an era that was less a war and more a rapid adoption of technologies, perceptions, bureaucratic processes, cultural norms, and globalist tendencies that converged under the banner of war.

The Global War on Terror did not take place. But you were there, a participant. Perhaps not of time or location but of consequence, surely. Come, I will show you.

Come and see.

>>> *END OF TRANSMISSION._*

---

1. I posit that we now inhabit a post-GWOT Era, where the hallucination of violence is deeply rooted in the social and political spaces that have coalesced between ignorance and indifference. The fever dream of violent acts we vicariously experience within the boundaries of our own nation feels increasingly similar to the low boil of day-to-day life endured by U.S. soldiers in Afghanistan during the GWOT. One need only look to the media and to daily streams of publicly available blotter data recorded by law enforcement, often compiled by the same software applications that cataloged our wars abroad. This is not to suggest that this default disarray, this "violence as content," is entirely grounded in truth or entirely manufactured (who can say?), but rather that our collective fight-or-flight response may never again be eased. From a purely bureaucratic standpoint, the "forever wars" never ended. The budgets remain intact, as do the personnel, the processes, and the will.

2. While reading this book, you may also discover, as I did in writing it, the techniques at play in the communications of Empire. The liberal application of adverbs in analysis and policy writing dilutes the finality of proclamation, rendering attribution and consequence less likely. Passive voice, or the "past exonerative tense" (as it is more appropriately referred to by those criticizing the media's whitewashing of state-sanctioned violence), also serves to meet this end.

3. These pages are dense with concepts, many of which I expect to be at least partially foreign to the reader. While some will be made clear by the end of the book, others will require the application of research and critical thinking. Everything that follows has been placed with explicit intent.

My Father's Name Is Forgotten

"Soldiers. Soldiers. Bring it in, soldiers." Instructor Willow's lips pursed each time he repeated the word. The air that escaped his mouth projected a high-pitched voice, dripping with indignation toward the recruits gathered before him.

"Check it out, soldiers. Let's talk about your assignments after basic. Overseas assignments are the best—you better hope you get one, soldiers. There's more money, the food's great, and those foreign women... they sure do love the uniformed man." Instructor Willow paused in reverent contemplation, reminiscing about moments that likely never occurred.

Young recruits sat cross-legged; some leaned against the dead pines, while others did their best to mimic the sure-footed stance of their new paternal guide. A vivid transference of values and social credit shook loose the taboos of youth; an ethos permeated the gathering—the Black Mass. Amazed stares and open hearts, unaware that their muzzles were being rubbed in shit.

The soldier's memories of Land Assault Force basic training, days spent in the SOF-T simulators, and Instructor Willow's stories had left them with a unique nostalgia, although its scent had gone rancid in recent months. A line formed to enter the armory at Company Headquarters, beckoning a familiar sense of dread to gnaw at the soldier's center of gravity.

Alpha Company HQ wasn't much to look at, with its brown roof and sickly mustard-colored exterior walls that mirrored the other structures along the strip. A dark tan sign—*A CO. 58th LAF BN - WAR HOUNDS*—swayed against a backdrop of manicured grass, the letters fading under an oppressive sun. As the line of War Hounds snaked into the basement, the soldier shuffled along in silence, staring at barren corridors of solid concrete blocks painted over in a drab white.

Waiting like this had become second nature. There was no particular use for this "free" time, and the appeal of a wandering mind had long been staved off by the rod. Instead, the soldier greeted a black void, a blank space behind the eyes in which events passed and the pressure of current circumstances could be abated.

Light returned just before reaching the armory window, then sound shortly after. Sergeant Wright, the company armorer, sat hunched over in a dim closet of a room, his pupils wide with stimulant, fingers clacking away at a number pad.

"How's it going, Sergeant?" The soldier droned out the greeting with just enough restraint and false motivation so as not to promote unnecessary interaction.

"Another day, another dollar—" The armorer began his reply on autopilot but shifted abruptly as his eyes darted to the soldier. "Well, if it isn't NOON-ES! How's my favorite female trigger puller?"

She remained impassive, though her eyes flashed with a hint of recoil. Instructor Willow had coined the moniker 'Noon-es'; unfortunately, it remained clinging to the soldier's heels long after basic training. Butchering surnames was practically a competitive sport for instructors who sought to remind young recruits of their newfound condition. As a soldier in the LAF, the legacy, culture, and personal meaning tied to one's name were subject to erasure. In their place, unit cohesion and duty were deliberately cultivated. After enough repetition of misnomers and epithets, one's true name would be reduced to no more than a label—a mere data point to set soldiers apart on the battlefield.

"I'm fine, Sergeant," she said as she touched her finger to a sensor mounted on the wall.

"I hear you're going out on mission today." The armorer glanced back and forth between the soldier and his screen. "I could always tell you were one of the good ones—not just here for the benefits. We need more trigger pullers like you; the softies seem to get worse every year." The armorer produced a mechanical glove, its index finger missing, and gave it a light toss to her. "Your suit's in Hangar Four today. You'll be marched to the flightline from there."

The soldier found her way out of the building and toward the hangars at the end of the street, slipping the glove on as she walked. The device activated at once, dulling most of the nerves in her right hand, leaving only her trigger finger to fidget in the early morning heat. Hangar Four's doors were parted halfway, revealing the SOF-T lockers and a gathering of her fellow War Hounds.

Soldier of the Future - Tactical was the latest in a long line of weapons programs aimed at enhancing Land Assault Force capabilities by pushing the limits of human-machine integration. The mechanical suits provided superior threat detection and risk mitigation for those encased inside, while an advanced software suite ensured accurate target identification and supported battlefield maneuvering. Most military jobs were automated into obsolescence long ago, but the law still mandated involving a human brain in the single decision associated with kinetic operations.

The program's name was a mouthful, but it served two distinct purposes. First, it satisfied the War Department's fantasies of *operating in the future of warfare*. The second, less official, was to provide every crusty non-commissioned officer with endless fodder for criticizing the quality of the latest generation of LAF recruits.

"All right, softies, get your asses in those suits!" a voice echoed throughout the hangar. The soldier couldn't tell whether it belonged to a human superior or one of the many disembodied Artificial Instructors that would accompany her from this point onward. Her slight twitch of an eye roll went unnoticed by the overhead surveillance system. Whirring fans and tired motors bled electric noise as each of the SOF-Ts initiated its boot sequence.

"HURRY... UP!"

She raised her gloved hand to a small aperture protruding from her locker. The oath-like motion triggered the container's unlocking mechanism, peeling away the front panels to reveal the suit inside.

The pride of the LAF stood splayed apart before the soldier, welcoming her back after four days of separation that had felt like mere minutes. She backed into the locker, stepping into the suit's legs, while a series of system and weapon function checks ran on the screen beside her. The upper half of the SOF-T bent forward at the hips, initiating the process of encasing her in two mechanical shells. The inner shell, a skin-tight composite, secured itself at key points: the ribs, under the arms, and between the legs. A bright white facemask sealed this inner layer, narrowing her vision through two eyeholes. The outer shell then collapsed around her, forming yet another protective layer capped with a dull yellow visor. Pneumatic bolts raced along the seams, anchoring her head, neck, and right hand into place.

Her eyes drifted up as she resigned herself. *I'm so fucking tired of this shit—*

Aerosolized droplets burst from the mask, peppering her face. She breathed in, a sharp gasp igniting flames laying claim to the mind, her pupils widening to take in every bit of light and activity the eyeholes in her mask could afford. Simultaneously, her body went limp below the sternum. One contractual requirement of the SOF-T platform included the need to protect the "decision-maker" while the suit performed automated and demanding battlefield maneuvers. Early operational testing revealed that only pliable bodies could withstand the machine's movements.

The effects of the aerosol and the pressure of the suit's inner shell limited her range of external stimuli to only those she could perceive through her eyes, ears, and right index finger. A small sensor rested millimeters away from the exposed digit, awaiting her slightest command.

The machine hummed with life.

"Another day in paradise, soldier! Soldier, I hope you're ready for this operation today, soldier." Instructor Willow's pitch, speech patterns, and condescension had been distilled and encoded as her personalized artificial battlefield mentor.

"I'm checkin' your readiness levels, soldier," AI Willow announced. The soldier seized upon a slight pause to brace her ears.

"What the FUCK are these alcohol readings, soldier?!"

The scream reverberated through her skull, triggering the usual and immediate dulling of her hearing, followed by an acute ring.

"You're lucky these blood-alcohol levels are still within regulations, soldier!"

She had grown accustomed to these toothless lashings. No matter how inebriated she got, she never quite achieved outright rejection.

"You know what? I got somethin' for that. You're pulling rear security for the others today, NOON-es. If there are triggers to pull and bodies to drop, it won't be you gettin' that action."

Rear security duty again. Maybe I'll get a full six hours tonight.

A rifle thrust out from a compartment in the locker's wall. The suit's maneuver algorithms took over, directing it to accept the weapon and march out of the hangar, falling in behind the other War Hounds.

A pair of transport aircraft hovered on the flightline, their autonomous pilot software emulating the poise and accuracy of hummingbirds. The sound and heat produced by the running engines constituted a force that would otherwise overwhelm a typical human, yet could not penetrate the outer shell of the suit. As the SOF-Ts approached, the rear ramps of the aircraft lowered, revealing gaping maws trimmed with dimly lit red lights. Each leaped one by one, clearing the five-meter gap with ease. The soldier tried not to think about how her joints would feel once her legs were returned to her.

She flinched as her suit locked into place along the inner fuselage, a necessity given the extreme gravitational forces troop transports could expect to endure. As combat operations transitioned to the autonomous era, the micromanagement of resources and the efficient use of time arose as the pillars of encoded LAF doctrine. Automated repetition gave way to innovation, initially significant but eventually minute and unnoticeable. The milliseconds shaved from each loading and unloading of the aircraft, each suit's ability to acquire targets, and the machine interface's capacity to elicit reactions from the soldier inside, represented the metrics by which LAF bureaucrat-generals would measure improvement. The operator was aptly identified as the key limiting factor to automation's progress, but even this could be reconciled.

A happy jingle played in the soldier's helmet as the ramp closed. ♫ *Hm-hmmmmm—No. Fuck that.*

The interior surface of her visor lit up, displaying a virtual classroom similar to those encountered during basic training. An instructor appeared, identifiable by their signature black cap. Their blurred face forced the soldier's now hyperaware brain into a vain loop, seeking interpretation and familiarity.

"I know you're not doing this for yourself, soldier." The virtual entity's words vibrated through her helmet and along contact points with the bone. "You need to think about the soldiers to your left and right when you're out there today. If you hesitate to pull that trigger, you will be responsible. It behooves you to think about that."

There would be no rest. The string of lectures, LAF promotional videos, and inhalant drugs would see to that. If any of her comrades were succumbing to madness, she wouldn't know. Internal communication links between suits were disabled years ago. As with all the others before it, this journey would pit her against that version of herself longing for an alternate reality, for that "what-if."

The joints in the SOF-T began to buckle and creak against gravity, signaling a final descent. As the rear ramp cracked open, natural light pierced through mental fog. The soldier squinted momentarily before the suit could react and dim the surface of her helmet, allowing her to glance over at the suit directly across. She didn't know who was inside, only that together they were the last two to board and would be the first out. With a groaning jolt, her suit detached from the safety harness and sprinted toward the exit.

By her estimate, the leap out was steeper than average, at least fifteen meters. She shut her eyes to avoid a mental panic, as the rest of her body was incapable of registering the experience. Upon hitting the ground, a cloud of orange dust kicked up, adding to the storm that the arrival of the aircraft had summoned. The suit sprang to action, readying its rifle and scanning the sector facing out from the exit ramp. The first suit to join her on the landing zone faced the opposite direction, focusing on the village toward which they would advance.

WARNING: PROBABLE WEAPON SYSTEM DETECTED - SMALL ARMS
- 2250m.

The message flashed across her visor, accompanied by a bounding indicator box highlighting the location of the threat.

She strained her eyes, but they proved rather useless at this distance.

The fuck is this? Already?

RECOMMENDED COURSE OF ACTION: ENGAGE

"Soldier, what the FUCK are you waitin' for, soldier?" AI Willow said. "Do you know how vulnerable your fellow soldiers are right now? You need to cover them AND the aircraft! SHOOT that fucker!"

Fuck—

The soldier's jaw clenched as her brain sent a single impulse to her finger. The isolated bundle of nerves responded, having long ached at the opportunity to interact with anything.

AUTHORIZATION - NUNEZ, J. - ENGAGING

The gesture, the flashing confirmation message, and the rifle firing all happened concurrently. As the rifle barrel dispersed a plume of gas and heat, another small cloud of dust powdered the air. The target indicator flashed and danced, straining to reacquire and assess through the haze of minerals.

CONDUCTING BATTLE DAMAGE ASSESSMENT... 1x ENEMY KIA.

SCANS COMPLETE. TOTAL ENGAGEMENT TIME: 15.34s

"Good job, soldier. I knew you had what it took to protect your fellow War Hounds. Your actions in accurately assessing the battlefield situation reflect well upon you and the LAF. Continue the mission." AI Willow's parental tone snaked into her ear, bearing silver pieces.

The scent of lavender filled her mask—*Mom's bedroom.*

Are my ears still ringing? No, that sounds like a crowd cheering.
She couldn't help but recall the personal pride she associated with events such as her high school graduation, completing her first marathon, and receiving her assignment orders to Alpha Company. She allowed these feelings of comfort and belonging to salve her anxieties and enter the void. Details of this initial engagement, including the suit's acquisition time, rifle accuracy, and the operator's hesitance to react, were relayed through the reconnaissance aircraft circling overhead.

Stillness returned to the air as the last War Hounds struck the earth. The soldier blinked through the leash that had so effectively maintained her undivided attention, revealing a swirling landscape of low mountains, cracked mud, and decaying shrubs. What value there ever was in the dirt had been extracted decades ago. All that remained was heat and hostility—a cynical greeting further filtered through the yellow film coating her visor. The atmosphere was reminiscent of the gritty war films her grandfather had been engrossed in during his latter years.

On the move. The suit shifted to keep pace with the others on their way to the objective, its sensors at work scanning for any threats that might approach the group from behind. Marching forward in reverse proved strenuous on the soldier's mind the first time she pulled rear security. Her comrades didn't secure her safety as much as the algorithms driving their movements and guiding their decisions. Coping with the mental fatigue of this position required a choice: Enthusiastically trust the invisible hand or embrace the meaninglessness of it all.

Still, she allowed herself to notice faint rays of hope, ashen though they were. Whatever brutality she might face here likely paled compared to what was unfolding out of view. The suit performed exceptionally in blocking the audio cues accompanying the "violence of action" SOF-T units were so well known for.

A flash of blue light caught the soldier's eye, originating from the direction of whatever she had just engaged.

More of them? Her eyes fluttered as she sought guidance from the targeting system. The indicator locked onto the source of the light, only to blink away. A second flash—a red one—occurred several hundred meters to the left of the first, triggering a similar response from her scanners.

She demanded answers from her suit. "Hey, what is this shit?" More flashes. The pulses of light increased in frequency, eliciting a more rapid series of scans—still, nothing.

"Fuck! There's something out—"

Her words halted as her suit nosedived, the powdered earth rising to meet her visor.

SOLDIER WOUNDED. LEGS CRITICALLY DAMAGED. NOTIFYING MEDEVAC. ETA FOR RECOVERY… END OF MISSION

She froze. *Oh god, what's wrong with my legs?* Her brain reacted as if undergoing a start-up sequence, reaching out to each limb, only to be left without a return. The suit dispersed another burst of aerosol, applying a false calm that no amount of alcohol or self-care could reproduce.

"Soldier, you're going to be okay, soldier. Take a knee and drink water," AI Willow's unfortunate voice pierced the bliss. "Need you ... in there ... medevac ... soon ..." The communication broke up and departed her altogether, as did the artificial illumination from her visor. Specks of dirt began to shroud the natural light filtering into the suit, encroaching on what little sense of focus remained.

"You still alive?"

An unfamiliar voice squelched through a previously non-functioning speaker positioned behind the soldier's right ear. The words conveyed no feeling, but she encountered a whisper of solace in the voice's accent, which resonated vaguely like her grandfather's.

"I'm going to need you to say something and let me know you're still there."

She managed a grunt through her mask, which had begun digging into her temples.

"Yeah, sorry about that. I had to let the suit do its thing with the medicine—can't be taking any chances. Your legs are fine, by the way, but for the time being, I own you. So, let's have a chat until your ride shows up."

The soldier forced a brief sigh. *My legs are okay. I'm okay. Fuck, where is everyone?*

"Did you see who it was that you killed just a few minutes ago? Surely you didn't have a positively identified target at that distance," the stranger said.

Her initial instinct was to stand behind the accuracy of her suit's targeting system and the apparent, non-coincidental combination of circumstances she faced upon her arrival. However, beneath the veneer of her instilled LAF values and creeping beyond the memories of her accomplishments, her recollections of battlefield engagements stood adamant and explicit, dredged up by the stranger's words and desperately seeking her attention.

"I gave her the callsign *Veleda*, but to be honest, I don't know who she was beyond her tribal affiliation—just some nomad driven to my organization by poverty and ignorance. We employ them to monitor and report your activities or transport our weapons. Veleda assisted with the equipment I used to hack your suit. Too bad there's nothing left of her for her family to mourn. I'm sure you can get a medal for this, though, right? She's a combatant in the eyes of your leaders. No harm, no foul."

The soldier envisioned the family she had dismantled: a woman and child, a few elders, all faceless, huddled around a fire and drinking tea.

"The others you arrived with will soon share in her misfortune. I figure we have about thirty minutes before the rest of your unit is dealt with, triggering an automated mass-casualty recovery by your headquarters. It still baffles me that no human up there gets word one way or the other until a computer decides you've crossed some exhaustively defined threshold. I bet your officers are too busy jerking themselves off to care."

The methodical, cold timbre of the stranger's voice was grating on the few nerves she maintained a connection with. It was the voice of someone who had experienced too much to mind, whose trust in all things had eroded with the events of each passing day. Her growing nihilism raged to match the flattened affect reaching her ear.

"Why don't you just kill me, too?" The words left the soldier's drug-parched lips with false conviction. It was her first time speaking to another human while in a suit.

"Because we know that the enemy always puts their poorest performers in the rear, just like we knew that you'd be left behind the moment you were disabled," the voice said with disgust. "We know you can't be all that bad, and this isn't entirely your fault. In fact, it's evidence that you're equipped with a bit more brain power than those comrades of yours. They're rats, exchanging a single impulse for gratification."

The voice sighed as a drill contacted the soldier's suit, boring a hole between the shoulder blades, a mechanized surgery to the symphony of invading hornets.

"What is this?! What are you doing to me?!"

"You know, these machines were originally built for manual operation. Take that inner shell you're wearing. It was designed to read your entire body and transmit its movements throughout the system. It didn't take but a minor software update to shift its function to what you experience now." The stranger's work pressed her visor further into the barren soil. "Your forces were far less predictable back then. Now? The algorithms micromanaging your movements are slaves to doctrine. Every action they take can be measured. And if they can be measured, they can be predicted and defeated."

"Goddammit, answer me!" she said.

"I'm here to give you a choice for once. We've watched as your military has increasingly relied upon the poor, the outcast, and the neurodivergent to satisfy its requirement for warm bodies. You come to them isolated, and they keep you that way. Meanwhile, they scan your brains in those simulators and figure out what scents, sounds, and images are necessary to ensure compliance."

Slight frustration blemished the man's words as he pulled at the soldier's suit, lifting her gaze a few inches above the dirt. "The few units in your armed forces still composed of humans are rife with abuse. I'm sure you've seen how those body-numbing drugs are used outside official operations, right? Then again, none of you seem to have social connections with your fellow soldiers. I'd be surprised that you'd know unless you encountered it firsthand." The source of his struggle gave way, reintroducing her to the minerals below.

She choked on her memories. Bonds were nonexistent in Alpha Company—competition and conflict provided all with the socialization deemed necessary. The environment fostered by her superiors bred a general indifference toward others. However, she couldn't help but notice the fleeting emotions her fellow War Hounds would occasionally allow to leak through: the anguish hidden behind laughter after returning from an operation, or once youthful expressions aged with resignation as they lined up outside their rooms, awaiting nightly inspections by the leadership. Her mask began applying such pressure that she feared it would fuse to the skin.

"Let me give you an idea of what exactly you'll face if you make it out of the LAF alive," he said. "You're not guaranteed to be physically whole, and you sure as hell won't come out mentally stable. Whatever substances you're consuming in private to counteract the suit's drugs will take you for a ride in the long run, while the same companies that built your suits will have subsidiaries welcoming you to their healthcare facilities with open arms." The stranger grunted as he sheared away metal components, fat trimmed from the meat. "The triggers they've used to hunt for your feelings of nostalgia will decay, and you will tirelessly chase after their shadows until your last days."

A loud metallic clang abused the soldier's eardrums as the stranger placed a device over the drill site. At that moment, she became more than a head and finger connected by crafted control. The introduction of consequence settled behind her pupils, its roots piercing the boundary between soldier and autonomous anonymity.

"Finding a steady job will be difficult," he continued, "and establishing lasting relationships will be damn near impossible.

Bits of that mask you're wearing now will continue to shine through, a warning to those around you to stay away."

The woman was flipped onto her back in a single, effortless motion. She winced at the silhouette of another suit, its features blotted out by the dirt particles still clinging to her helmet.

"The best part is the self-doubt you'll face after every interaction with another human. 'Is there something about me they don't like? Is it just me being paranoid again?'"

A mechanical hand wiped the dirt away from her visor, revealing a looming machine similar to hers in appearance, albeit with a transparent surface. A man peered down at her from within, his thick mustache lending further severity to stern features. His right eyelid hung loosely, with nothing of substance beneath.

"Are you going to wear that insecurity as a badge of honor, or will you let it isolate you in a stream of your own compulsions? Perhaps both? As much as I've tried, I can't admire the ingenuity of this weapon. I only see the arrogance of its creators. I see the greed of the manufacturers reflected in its vulnerabilities, the hubris of the analysts in every double-edged efficiency, and the apathy of the people you serve in the way this machine rewards violence."

A white flash erupted from the village, summoning a reflection that obstructed the man's face. His features did not flinch, nor did his eye wander.

"That's my cue." The stranger rested a hand on the woman's visor, his index finger over her eyes. "I'm going to return most of your suit's autonomous functions after I'm long gone. However, the device I've placed on your back can override it all. If you'd like, you can reset this machine's controls to manual. To activate it, give your trigger sensor a few taps like this."

She followed the finger as it made three quick beats, three prolonged beats, and then again, three quick beats.

"They're going to have to destroy your suit to stop it. Before you make that decision, though, you should know that I've disabled the drug lines to your mask. You're going to feel every bit of that choice."

Her narcotic-induced daze was already beginning to fade. "What the fuck am I supposed to do with this? What makes you think I won't go back, finish this enlistment, and get the fuck on with my life?" she said.

"The way I see it, you can return to a society where the illusion of choice presents itself under the cloak of nostalgia, or you can choose to struggle against it and put this machine to good use. Hell, maybe I made everything up, and it's a bomb I've attached to you—poof. Either way, I'm alleviating your control issues, and you're doing me a service by striking back."

The stranger rose and pivoted away from the woman, kicking up dirt as he sprinted off. A final squelch from the speaker heralded the return of silence. She was alone again. The chemicals coursing through her veins, synthetic or otherwise, began to dilute and settle. She drifted, partly due to exhaustion but also out of habit. The unconscious mind, particularly one devoid of dreams, need not concern itself with choice.

Nuñez awoke to a wave of violent vibrations and the familiar dim interior lights of an LAF aircraft. No care had been taken to secure her in place, and the turbulence was forcing her suit to scrape along the floor. As the aircraft pitched, she collided with obscure objects strewn about the cargo bay. Her body, no longer numb, registered every impact as her muscles seized—a routine delivery of debris to the nearest LAF base.

The suit whimpered with renewed life. A jingle, this time triumphant, ruptured the silence as the aircraft descended.

It's not that simple. It's never been that fucking simple.

The rear ramp lowered, bathing Nuñez in twilight. Flesh and mechanical components littered the medevac's interior, the recoverable remains of Alpha Company.

Her visor lit up once again. AI Willow, having successfully rebooted, let out a bellow: "Another day in paradise, soldier!"

i. Our Relationship with "The Apocalypse"

There exists a recurring "novel" idea in our time that, given the examination of humanity's iterations throughout history, a pattern of generalization emerges: *Suffering is strength, both literal and moral, while prosperity is weakness.* Guided by this assumption, generations may be wholly characterized as good or bad, and the events they shape lead to the cyclical forging of one another. On its face, this belief appears marked by ancient knowledge, an edict solidified by the rise and fall of countless empires and ages, with behaviors and actions as predictable as the stars. In truth, this proclamation embodies the ideals of the apocalypse-fetishizing death cults that so willingly parrot it. It is wisdom for the ignorant, laced with tribalism, narcissism, and cynicism. It presents a construct within which people may mask their responsibilities and behaviors, shirking any duty to build more, to be better.

Thinking positively, simplistically, and generationally, there are two general archetypes, both capable of traversing a moral spectrum: the Explorer and the Caretaker.[1] These roles aren't tied to consecutive generations, societal norms, or the success/failure dynamic, but rather to necessity. The Caretakers establish and consolidate the means by which Explorers may seek opportunity.[2] Socioeconomic conditioning has resulted in an environment within which the individual is fanatically convinced of their role as an Explorer, a baseless title demanding participation in consumerism, nostalgia, and demagogy, as well as the seemingly virtuous or obligatory ideals that serve to cloak these three sirens. Those aspiring Caretakers who stood resolute during humanity's transition to the digital age have since become disillusioned and effectively neutered by insurmountable inequity. Furthermore, the sacrifice required to perform this necessary role is increasingly the subject of taboo and cynicism.

At any given time, someone, somewhere in this world, is facing down "The Apocalypse." It persists in the form of tyrannical leaders, conflicts, natural disasters, societal upheavals, "signs" from god(s), and any combination thereof. It has been this way and will continue to be this way so long as there remains someone left still restrained by the basest evolutionary desires to seek and address threats of complexity, especially in cases where none genuinely exist as perceived.[3] In truth, no matter what obstacles we face, humanity will find a way to continue, at least in mind, if not body. At an individual level, a communal level, and a societal level, the courageous must seek answers that are the most responsible to the future. Caretakers cannot be left bankrupt of resources, knowledge, or understanding, nor can Explorers proceed without a Foundation.

Belief in the Cult of The Apocalypse has, time and time again, halted generational progress, made stagnant the critical thinking necessary to adapt to inexplicable change, and laid waste to time and our relationship with it.

---

1. In revisiting this idea, I had thought of a third archetype: the Survivor. However, a Survivor can also be considered a Caretaker, albeit with a scope of influence that is limited by circumstance and environment, among other factors.

2. People are capable of embodying both archetypes, perhaps living within one over the other during a given period in their lives. However, one's capacity to inhabit these archetypes is increasingly subject to influences and desires perpetuated by both markets and the state.

3. Apophenia, a common tendency to perceive connections to which one assigns an abnormal meaning, is an interesting phenomenon that should be understood in relation to this topic. It is a natural, albeit biased, thought process that, in its extreme form, is a symptom of paranoid schizophrenia. The gambler's fallacy is an example of this tendency, a phenomenon gaining increasing relevance as corporations continue to blur the line between play and financial consequence. Mass apophenia is a condition that is frequently sought out and cultivated in state disinformation campaigns. Algorithms seed the fields in which conspiracy grows.

And Hades Followed Him

"Good evening, sir. What can I do you for?" A soiled apron draped off the man's barrel-chested frame. His thinning black curls, dampened by the heat of the kitchen, were mostly contained under a black ball cap emblazoned with a double-headed eagle. The scent of garlic had made a permanent dwelling of the deep creases in his skin and under the nails, compulsive handwashing be damned. It was a slow afternoon, not at all uncommon in the remnants of former Greektown. The American Dream had marched along in its indefinite iterations, as it tends to do, and Haralambis Ypsilantis was resistant to change, as we tend to be.

The restaurant's lone customers were a rather bulbous and unhealthy-looking couple, presumably in their late fifties. Blood-red pores stretched across bloated, pale skin, choked off by smog and wildfire ash. They had lived well enough that their excesses had taken a measurable toll but were not so old yet as to be humbled by frailty. The gentleman flipped a double-sided menu several times, expecting to see something different with each laborious motion.

"Yeah, can I have your Greek salad? But instead of a Greek salad, can you just make it a Caesar salad?"

"Yeah... no. We don't do that here, I'm afraid." Haralambis' stare extended through the customer's face and bored into the tile floor. *Kseftilismeno! The audacity of these broke-dick, no-class-havin'-ass-mother—*

"Well, all right, I suppose that's just the Greek way. I'll have the Greek salad. No olives, please." The man's light sarcasm flailed about, a rusted blade in the hands of a petulant child.

"Greek salad. No. Olives." Haralambis' eyes shifted to the man's wife, his heavy stubble exposing the aggression behind his strained smile. "And for you, ma'am?"

The man answered, "Oh, she'll have the same as me. We have to be watching our girlish figures, don't we?"

"Hey, Theo!" Haralambis said. "Two Greek salads! No olives."

A young man's eyes peered back from the kitchen, an amused smile forming once again at his uncle's expense. "Sure thing, *Barba* Haris."

An old flatscreen on the back wall featured a live news stream. Troubles in the Western Balkans, having raged over the last decade, had finally spilled over into parts of Europe yet reluctant to relinquish the privilege of patronizing their southern neighbors. Stock tickers marched along the bottom of the screen to the tune of flagrant tech buzzwords and the ever-growing arms trade.

With one ear tuned to the day's events, the older man leaned over the table toward Haralambis, doing his best to portray the mobsters he'd only witnessed in film. "They wouldn't be having these problems if Clinton had bombed the right people back in Kosovo, don't you think?"

"I remember seeing plenty of shitheads on all sides only a few years ago."

"You were there with the Greek military?"

"The American one."

"Well, I figured as you're Greek—"

"My family's been American for over a hundred years."

The man paused. Mock duty overwhelmed his drifting confusion, and he blurted, "Thank you for your service."

"Sure."

"Say, you're fellow Christians, right? What do they think in your congregation? Are we in the End Times?"

Haralambis glanced at the television. "Someone is."

"I'm willing to bet enough of your people think so. I heard there's one of those doomsday structures around here. You know anything about that?"

"Can't say I do, no."

"I suppose not. We're no billionaires. No wealth. No connections. Not that I mind, though. We hold no yearnings for escape. We're ready. Aren't we, sweetie?"

The man's wife nodded.

Haralambis joined his nephew out of earshot in the kitchen. He broke the young man's concentration with his half-serious chiding. "I swear to God, Theo. As your *nonós*, I forbid you from letting this country turn you into one of these clowns."

Theo picked up a jar of olives, only to place it back on the counter, just out of reach. "How am I supposed to do that?"

"Hm. That's a good question, little homie. You can start by doing the exact opposite of what I did."

"Marrying a Greek woman?"

"Letting your parents tell you who you can and can't marry. Allowing your community to dictate who you need to be or what you need to buy to fit in—those go hand in hand around here. Inviting anyone to speak to you of unquestionable truths. And don't believe for a second the discount dreams that they will try to sell you while you're still young. I wasted my time and health digging for lint in Uncle Sam's pockets."

Theo finished the salads with slices of feta, his movements deliberate. "Maybe you need more luck."

"Maybe luck isn't enough anymore. For too long, your *mamá* held the thin veil of opportunity that shielded your eyes from consequence. I've known so many less fortunate than us. One day, you'll understand." *That great wall of sand on the horizon, greeting you every morning. Sometimes, it's closer, sometimes further, but it's always there. The people out there, perhaps they knew Consequence once—watched as she applied the rod to those deserving. They have forgotten. They pray for an end, unaware of the will that will mete out that force.*

"The sooner that day comes, the sooner I'll know all that you know, Barba," Theo said as he loaded the salads onto a tray and left the kitchen.

Then I pray it waits.

"Here you are. Two salads, no olives," Theodoros said.

"Thank you! These look great, don't they?" The man couldn't be bothered to seek the acknowledgment on his wife's face.

"Is there anything else that you need?" Theodoros said.

"How long have you been working here for your family?"

"I've been helping my uncle each summer since he came back three years ago. He took over the restaurant for my grandparents."

A flash of movement caught Theodoros' eye. A disheveled, overly dressed woman hobbled past the restaurant's windows that overlooked Main Street. Gaudy amounts of silver reflected the afternoon sun, calling attention to the woman's hands, neckline, and ears. A young child was bundled in one arm; a suitcase hung from the other, which bumped into the back of her leg as she struggled to maintain a consistent pace.

"Well, they're lucky to have you," the man said. "I can't rely on my kids to make a phone call, much less work for me. Just hope they don't have you singin' any slave songs back there." The man's expression anticipated familiarity, as if he were conversing with an old friend.

Theodoros experienced a blank pause. *What the hell does that even mean?* He forced a chuckle and a nod as he turned away to head back to the kitchen.

"Is it your church that maintains the shelter nearby?" The man's tone was more serious.

"They support the homeless shelter down on Twelfth, but I think the city runs that," Theodoros said.

"Oh, I'm not talking about that," the man said with a laugh. "I mean that big underground structure your people have for the End Times. They've got 'em all over the country now, but this one's the closest to our property."

"I'm not sure what you're—"

"Of course you do! You've noticed the shady construction, the big, rolling covers. Recent happenings have all these rich folk performing hasty inspections. They crave that peace of mind that only we saved have found."

Barba Haris' voice echoed from the kitchen, "Theo! I need some help with the spit rotisserie!" There was an unfamiliar distress in his words.

Deep lines formed on Theodoros' forehead as he looked over his shoulder toward the kitchen. *We don't have a spit.* He turned back to the man. "Uh… sorry, it's a two-person job handling that thing."

The man's lips pursed. "Don't let me keep you from tending to your duties. I'll give you some time to think about it."

In Theodoros' absence, Barba Haris had removed his apron, donned a hoodie, and was speed-walking between the kitchen and the storage closet.

"What's this about?" Theodoros said.

Barba Haris' voice was hushed, direct, robotic. "Get your backpack and empty it. We have two minutes."

"What do you mean? Are we closing? I'll go tell the customers—"

"Don't." Barba Haris slouched forward, ensuring he could look at Theodoros directly. "Just focus on what I tell you to do, all right, little homie? Get your backpack and fill it with this bread." The muscles in his face bulged from jaw to temple.

Theodoros retrieved his bag from the closet and dumped its contents on the kitchen floor. A copy of Thucydides' *History* landed atop the pile.

Barba Haris briefly examined Theodoros' belongings. "Keep the book. Fill the rest with bread."

"It's just a book for class."

"Not anymore, it isn't."

Barba Haris finished readying his bag before quietly shuffling Theodoros out the restaurant's back door and onto a back street where his car was parked.

"Let's hope we make it in time," Barba Haris said as he started the engine and navigated his vehicle onto the street parallel to the town's center.

The vehicle accelerated rapidly. Theodoros gripped the car door, clammy fingers slipping along the cheap plastic. Barba Haris would lightly decelerate just before each intersection, only to lurch forward again as Theodoros caught his breath. Looking at his uncle, Theodoros caught glimpses of Main Street every few hundred feet.

Outside the laundromat, a woman was fighting her three uncooperative children, pleading on the verge of tears that they submit to a few hours of boredom. A group of young people around Theodoros' age was posing by a large fountain, surrounded by adoring family. Their brightly colored dresses reflected a deep pride transacting the role that the *quinceañera* would inherit this day. Life burned steadily out there while Barba Haris roared of the furnace.

"Tell me what's going on!" Theodoros said.

"An attack. A big one. I got an alert on my phone. The community pays extra for that. Subscription service—a heads-up before the news stations catch on."

"What? Who's attacking?"

"I don't know."

"Where are we going?"

"The place that donkey back at the restaurant kept asking about. There's something the community had built underneath that big-ass lot next to the church. Construction ended not long after you were born."

"Where we do the festival?"

"Exactly," Barba Haris said. He placed his hand on Theodoros' shoulder, giving it a heavy pat while his attention remained fixed ahead. "Look at you, asking the five Ws! Proud."

"Can we stop at home for something?"

"No." Barba Haris continued scanning. "Look, today's going to be difficult, Theo. I want you to get a good look at the sky, the sun, the grass, these people. Take a good sniff of the bread. Study your reflection. The trauma will etch those experiences into your memory. I wish I could've done the same. I'd take bread and sunlight over shit and dirt."

Theodoros looked ahead at the road. It appeared to narrow each time Barba Haris swerved through an intersection. He felt the seat belt slide along his shoulder and cut into his neck. His gaze fell to the car's dashboard, its leather-like texture offering up all the faux patterns his mind craved in the moment.

"Fuck," Barba Haris said, sighing.

The vehicle slowed. Theodoros glanced up to see a world that had caught up with his uncle's urgency—surpassed it, even. A collective thought that, having failed to make immediate sense of the horizon, defaulted to the throes of the inferno.

"We're walking from here, Theo," Barba Haris said. "Little under a mile. Wear your bag on your chest, keep your head down, and stay next to me. Walk with a purpose, little homie."

As Theodoros exited the car, he could not help but experience the temptations of the chaos unfolding around him. Vehicles mired, their drivers raging with horns and screams and gestures. A family exits a nearby business and breaks into a sprint, not realizing that they've left their youngest behind on the street. The moment subsided as Barba Haris appeared at his side, placed a large hand on the back of his neck, and steered him while walking toward the church.

"I got us," Barba Haris said as he kept Theodoros' attention on their feet. Against the cacophony of desperation unfolding, Barba Haris' words illuminated a path. "Your *yiayia* used to tell me stories that her yiayia would tell her about the years before she came to this country. She and other women of the village were hidden and smuggled during the occupation, barely a step ahead of the invaders. She was young, around your age, and faced a much worse fate than we do now. I find myself reflecting on her circumstances. What convinced her to leave it all behind? Why did she choose this place? Was it luck? Instinct? Experience? Why did she move her feet while others chose to stay? I did not know her. I can only recognize that she adapted. Whether she chose the correct path or not, her decision resulted in us."

Barba Haris moved to cover Theodoros' eyes as they navigated a heap of automobile parts and flesh. Smoke scraped at the linings of their lungs and threatened to embed there—a would-be reminder of this tragedy.

"Right now, we move as she moved. Know as she knew," Barba Haris said between coughs. "Where we are going, there will be time to reflect on this."

Theodoros struggled to match his uncle's pace. His breathing lamented the need to press ahead, to reject failure before Barba Haris.

"It's all right, little homie. We're almost there. Switch your backpack around. I'll carry you."

Barba Haris lifted Theodoros with a fireman's carry, keeping his right hand free to swing near his hip. Theodoros remained silent, save for his rejections of the surrounding smoke. As he hung off his uncle's shoulders, Theodoros glimpsed the face of a man content with his place. Despite the strain of carrying Theodoros, Haralambis' stride was steady, perhaps even relishing the challenge. His state of mind was that of the forever sterile home, the door lock that never required a second and third inspection, the pair of hands unsullied.

Theodoros frowned. *How do I become like him?*

As they approached the church, Theodoros spotted a robed man guiding a child through a small opening in the festival lot's surface. The man turned toward them and, with a gentle smile, beckoned them over.

"Father Markos, we've made it," Barba Haris said as he slid Theodoros off his shoulders.

"And I thank God for it. Come, let's send you both down to join the others. We were lucky to have so many of the children here for dance rehearsal. I started lockdown procedures the moment the alert came through. There's not much time left."

"What about you? Do you need help getting inside?"

"I'm old, Haris. I won't make the trip, and I can't subject the children to seeing me that way."

Father Markos' eyes shifted away from Barba Haris and to the street. His panicked gasp called Theodoros' attention to the impending threat. A white pickup truck accelerated directly at them, its grill dented in and caked with blood.

"Get inside!" Barba Haris said, his arms scooping Theodoros and flinging him toward the entrance of the underground passage.

Theodoros stumbled down the first ten or so dimly illuminated steps before turning around. The stairwell echoed with screeching tires. Only Father Markos was visible at the entrance, his body rigid.

"You lied to me!"

The words reached Theodoros, who recognized them as belonging to the old man from the restaurant. He took a step up the stairwell, only to pause as Father Markos made a slight gesture, waving him off.

"Where's your wife, old-timer?" It was Barba Haris.

"I won't be left behind!"

Three shots rang out. Theodoros covered his ears and ducked. He looked up to see Father Markos doing the same.

Barba Haris approached Father Markos and handed him a pistol before wiping his hands on his hoodie. He received a shaky nod from the priest in return. Theodoros searched his uncle's silhouetted face for traces of what had transpired. The eyebrows were stretched upward from points along their outer edges, forming dark creases that mellowed at the center of the forehead. Unblinking eyes scanned Theodoros and beyond, tracing the present over agonizing sequences, carved pathways of the mind along which even the most mundane daily occurrences were forced to march. The hand of a beast writhed along the scalp, replacing logic with the first commandment of survival: See!

"We gotta go, Theo! We're not safe yet," Barba Haris said.

The grated steps felt wobbly beneath Theodoros' feet. Loose wires trailed down the pathway, connecting a series of small LED lamps.

"Typical," Barba Haris said with a chuckle. "I suppose the old goats had to cut their costs somewhere, though."

An automated message sounded faintly from further down the stairwell. Theodoros continued his descent while straining for the words. The voice cycled through several languages before making its way back to English.

"Launch status check initiated. Five minutes to lockdown."

"Double time, Theo!" Barba Haris said.

Theodoros felt the metal grating bite through his shoes as he raced down the steps. Ahead, a bright white door stood ajar. A foot extended out over the threshold from behind it.

"Don't close it yet!" Theodoros said.

As they approached, the door let out a low hiss, revealing a delicate woman heaving her body weight against steel and ceramic.

"We knew you were coming," the woman said after finishing with an accomplished grunt. She produced a handheld radio from her pocket. "Father Markos said two men would be joining to protect us during the journey. *Ela*. Ela. We must prepare."

Theodoros followed the woman into a small, circular chamber as Barba Haris closed the door behind them. Hydraulic locking mechanisms sounded, echoed by an announcement from the speakers overhead. Coffin-like structures lined the walls, with small apertures that allowed even smaller faces to study Theodoros as he was seated among them. He slipped into a large pair of rubberized pants attached to his seat. As he did so, the system inflated around his legs, applying small bursts of pressure to his thighs and calves.

"Cardiovascular maintenance calibrated."

Theodoros flinched as the announcement screeched from the speaker behind his headrest.

"I'm so sorry, *manari*. Let me fix that," the woman said. She adjusted a dial before swiping Theodoros' hair to the side and pulling down the cover of his chamber, encapsulating him. His eardrums pulsed, then attuned to the flows, beats, and squelches originating beneath the skin. Theodoros grimaced at the introduction, a profane awareness of vulnerability that clashed with his internalized identity of the body as machinery, its processes discreet, reliable, and uniquely isolated.

"Cover retraction."

The artificial luminescence dimmed as red sunset filtered in through windows that formed a ring above. Theodoros found

Barba Haris seated across the room. His lips were moving, but the shadows casting over his face rendered them unreadable.

"All right, manaria. It's Ms. Melpomene. Can you all hear me? Nod if you can hear me."

Theodoros eased his shoulders as the woman's voice vibrated at the back of his head.

"Listen to me, everyone. Listen to my breathing. Follow my breathing. You can close your eyes if you're scared. Follow along with—"

"Emergency launch."

A deafening roar tore through Theodoros' chamber, pressing his spine under an immense, numbing weight. His fingers jolted atop the armrests, only for their presence to fade again as he gripped the seat, his senses narrowing with the growing rumble. Flamelight flickered through the windows while black haze crept into his vision, retreating slowly as his legs were constricted.

Theodoros fixated on a single window above Barba Haris. The horizon was visible through it, streaked by plumes of unknown origin. Melpomene's further efforts to soothe were reduced to white noise. The room pitched forward, rotating the coastline into view countless miles below. Sparks raced into the sky, escaping the anvil ahead of the hammer's strike. Some were steady in their ascent, while others tumbled erratically before splitting apart, their glow fading into smoke. The structure groaned around Theodoros, a metallic tick-ticking that threatened a similar end as it slowed. Gravity sapped at his focus, pulling his eyes from the window and back to Barba Haris, who had grown exasperated in his attempts to signal an urge for control and calm.

Sunlight transitioned to earthlight as the tumult subsided. The internal systems rebooted, followed by a loud chime.

"We're safe for now, manaria," Melpomene said over the speakers.

Since entering space, a screen on the central console had flashed with a single message:

OLYMPUS MONS COLONY COORDINATES CONFIRMED.

Digital imagery accompanied it, depicting brilliant metallic structures set against red-orange powder—outdated renderings that Theodoros had been studying for days.

Barba Haris had recently completed another lesson, outlining his steps for developing a morning ritual that demanded efficiency and cleanliness above all. He floated over to Theodoros, his usual tension absent from his face and shoulders. "You're already obsessing over those? We just woke up."

"They're going to turn out like you, Barba," Theodoros said.

Barba Haris glanced over his shoulder at the children, who had set themselves upon developing a new tumbling routine, much to Melpomene's frustration. "In any other situation, I'd scream at myself for holding my anxieties as something to be learned from. But who knew a sardine can would prove the optimal environment?"

"Or survival, the optimal scenario?"

Barba Haris paused. "What's your impression of the colony?"

"I'd like to think there's room for us here, but something doesn't add up."

"Let's try broadening our perspective with a little exercise," Barba Haris said. "We are aware that the colony existed well before our launch. It's established and populated with the people who funded the colony and subsidized the escape fleet."

"Right."

"And you saw the large number of other capsules that barely made it off the ground before disintegrating. It was a bottleneck event."

"...Yes."

"Have we discussed mobility? In all its forms?"

"Mobility?"

"In the Army, we expended countless resources on maintaining what we called 'freedom of movement.' You need to spend to keep your routes open, cleared of threats, and traversable. Resources secure mobility. It is a privilege afforded to the haves and an illusion for have-nots. It is freedom of movement in physical space and within structures, with justice being one of the more prominent."

"So, we're here because we have mobility."

"We have no more mobility than the migrant crossing the desert on foot or braving the ocean via raft. The community had money, but they didn't have *money*." Barba Haris pointed upwards. "They want us. We're discounted bodies."

"Then we're to be indentured? The Constitution doesn't apply where we're going."

"That is my best guess, yes."

Theodoros' eyes narrowed. "Then why are we here? Sounds like we'd be better off having ended it back home!"

Barba Haris spoke in a hushed tone as he placed a hand on Theodoros' arm. "You assume I haven't thought of that, Theo?

Each night I strap into that coffin and close my eyes, I agonize about my decision."

"Then why?"

"I can't name any reasons that aren't selfish at heart. If we were to die anyway, I'd rather die with you having seen the stars. I couldn't forsake the struggles and sacrifices of those who came before us. I refuse to let these people enjoy the fruits of our culture without having a true product of it to answer to."

"You're starting to sound like *Pappou*."

"Perhaps he was right in this sense. As they sent me to war, it was not to the tune of the fife but to that of the *aulos*. I heard my father's praises in its notes, only for their meaning to fade amidst a hollow facsimile. They've repurposed our language into cute terms that they sprinkle throughout their religious practices. They've assimilated our cultural thought, only to denounce and corrupt it beyond recognition. They've worn our barbarism and courage like an ill-fitting mask. Now they sit on Mytikas, thinking they've escaped the problems they created! Kseftilismeni!"

Theodoros gave his uncle a light kick in the shin and motioned toward the children. They were blissfully unaware, caught in antigravity antics. "And what can we do about it?"

"We teach. We learn. We live. It's all we can do for now."

"Will we fight?"

Barba Haris drifted a few inches from Theodoros, his eyes unfocused and unblinking. He bumped into a handrail that protruded from the wall, and the jolt reset his thoughts. "I've never mentioned much about my pappou. He died when I was young—young enough that I never became aware of his flaws," Barba Haris smiled, "but old enough that he still imparted an impression of his character. And a character Pappou was. He was an engineer deep in his soul, and everyone learned that about him, one way or another. Everything to him was something to be quantified and solved. When the sickness came, he fought hard. I could tell. His mind... it was all numbers in the end. He was counting, running through the equations he had used since he was a young man... anything to maintain his grip on life as the rest of his body failed. I think about him often when I'm lost in routine. If I get that old, where will I go? I can't help but imagine I'll retreat to a far darker sanctuary."

Barba Haris opened a panel on the wall, revealing a semi-transparent viewing pane that was backlit and tinted in chlorophyll green. "Those renderings are missing the trash fields, where I assume they will expect us to toil. They don't depict the shambles we will be housed in." Barba Haris put an arm around Theodoros as they took in the light, recalling life in their homeland with a longing that was knowing in its permanence.

"Nor can they capture our opportunity."

ii. If You Know, You Know

The problem with the anti-war discourse since Vietnam is that it occasionally relies upon outright falsehoods, is often derisive and persecutory regarding ideas of both masculine and feminine identity, and is almost always too far up its own ass.

It should be clear by now that anti-war messaging has little to no effect on those who either directly or indirectly benefit from war's conduct. Furthermore, the consumption and voting patterns of individuals are so ensnared as to seem confined within a world entirely foreign to the machinations of the military-industrial complex. For those on the outside, there is but one singular point of influence: Who provides the bodies?

One does not reach prospective recruits, young people champing at the bit to find and express their purpose, by informing them of the hopelessness and stupidity of their decision. The military's messaging has effectively combatted that narrative for decades. Nor can one embellish the consequences of military service and conflict. Not only do the youth have a lack of tolerance for bullshit, but Hollywood is far more capable in its selling of tall tales rubber-stamped by the Pentagon.

In this case, those who have lived the experience are the most qualified to provide the details necessary to warn of its return.[1] Outside those families providing recruits generation after unflinching generation, most Americans espousing the benefits of military service do not have the exposure required to form a responsible opinion regarding war and its consequences. The GWOT generation's recruitment was bolstered by the societal shame of those fathers and grandfathers who could not or did not participate in the Vietnam War (materializing under the specter of both the draft and the achievements of The Greatest Generation), coupled with what was often the loudest voice in every household: the television.

It is a rare occasion when a veteran lends their words to speak against a major underpinning of our national mythos. It is simpler to market one's whitewashed memoir or repackage one's horrors as personal development, both exercises in vanity. Unfortunately, even when a memoir includes valid criticisms of war, it proves nearly impossible for the author to divorce the consequences of war from the identity and achievements they feel they've received during their service. The result is often an ill-conceived but well-intentioned publication of mixed messages, requiring a detailed understanding of nuance that may not be feasible. When a veteran fully commits to anti-war discourse, their words are quickly commodified and redistributed, generally alongside tired, weak narratives.[2] If their message relies on the accurate retelling of their past, they face an endless inquisition, likely pursued by members of their own community.[3] Dismissal is a natural consequence.

Disrupting the cycles of war requires difficult conversations held in the simplest and most intimate of locales: the dining table, the classroom, places of worship, and so on. If you are a veteran, do not follow your predecessors down the path of silence; it will only serve to further condemn the next generation. If you are not a veteran and want to help, share our unfiltered words *outside* your academic, social, and political circles, preferably with the *youth* who will be targeted for recruitment and those who will raise them. We will handle the rest.

1. It should be noted that veteran status does not confer immunity from a basic tenet of analysis: Consider the source. When considering the validity of a veteran's viewpoint (or any viewpoint, for that matter), you should account for factors such as economic incentive (is their priority to sell a narrative, tell a story, or something else?), ideological slant (are they supporting the interests of an adversary to the U.S. government, or is that merely a convenient perception?), and ego (are they pursuing a vendetta, boasting, etc.?).

2. Anti-war narratives are often co-opted by the state, serving dual purposes. They may be utilized to discredit adversarial war efforts abroad while, through the implicit acknowledgment of hypocrisy, simultaneously dissuade anti-war discourse at home. The co-opting of anti-war discourse allows the state to maintain a firm grip on the club, a tool of policy that is both too simple and too familiar to relinquish.

3. As much as I acknowledge the potential disservice involved in highlighting mental health as a relevant factor in this analysis, I cannot exclude it. As we currently understand them, disorders such as PTSD are, by definition, marked by symptoms such as suspiciousness and memory loss, which have the potential to contribute further bias to discourse. One method to combat this bias is to seek accounts from multiple sources. Collecting the stories of those non combatants who have survived war may allow for a more balanced perspective.

Chasing the Dragon

Yesterday, we began interrogations of the prisoners taken during our recent operation in Khashek village. Most were unresponsive to our methods or had little useful information regarding enemy positions. One prisoner, a man not yet twenty, required quarantining after our interrogator uncovered the presence of a skin condition on his wrists and neck. The prisoner appeared to be under the influence of narcotic substances and, in his daze, shifted between rage and terror as he described encountering a "great serpent" at the base of the mountain range to the north. We had a good laugh at his expense. Our comrades in Bamyan Province reported hearing a similar story, likely a holdover myth from the time before Islam supplanted its competitors as the opiate of choice.

This morning, we found the prisoner unresponsive. His body radiated energy; it was unlike anything I had previously encountered in a human. He had become a super-heated machine of flesh, reminding me of the BMP-1 engines we would huddle around during the early days of the invasion. We burned the body, much to the dismay of the other prisoners. Despite the wishful complaints of the more junior soldiers, the commander has refused to quarantine the unit—we are still needed to support the mission. After all, this is merely one threat among many in a land that seeks to swallow us with each misstep.

Capt Aleksandr Kusharev
191ˢᵗ Separate Motor Rifle Regiment
Ghazni Province, Afghanistan
28.03.81

Zana Khan District Outskirts
Ghazni Province, Afghanistan
15 APR 2011 - 1512Z

Sunset over Ghazni. A chill clung to the air, begging Spring to wait a bit longer. Rising temperatures would soon bring an end to the poppy season, as well as beckon the return of widespread, oversaturated violence—the Fighting Season. A lone Blackhawk helicopter navigated the horizon, a near-insignificant point moving along a vast, jagged plateau toward the province's northern mountains. The stillness of the expanse was lost on the Blackhawk's occupants: a pilot, copilot, and ten operators, all of whom were eager to get off the FOB and back to doing something, anything resembling that which they had been trained to do. Captains "Mac" McLoughlin and

"Andy" Schaeffer were bullshitting, as per tradition, without a care in the world.

Mac's voice crackled over the internal comms link. "Hey Andy, did I tell you about the first time I met Sergeant Major?"

"No, man, what happened?"

"So, it's a Thursday before a four-day, and I'm helping some of my soldiers clean the office so they can leave early."

"See, that's where you went wrong."

"Yeah, well, I'm pushing this old-ass vacuum to the supply closet. I round this corner and nearly run the Sergeant Major over. He says, in his crazy Texan accent, 'LT, where are you from?'"

"Oh, you have fucked up now."

"I say, 'California, Sergeant Major.' He pauses a second, long enough for me to consider ending it all, and says, 'That's why,' and pops smoke."

Andy chuckled. "Well, you know what they say about guys from California…"

"That they're welcome at your mom's house?"

"Hey now, motherfucker." Andy's barely discernible smile betrayed his serious tone.

"Five mikes out," the copilot said.

Two days prior, village elders from Khashek provided a substance of unknown biological origin to a U.S. Army patrol conducting a routine key leader engagement. The villagers reported discovering the substance, at the time encased in a pressure cooker and several plastic bags, in a *karez* system connecting a nearby satellite village to the northern mountains. While extended droughts had rendered the ancient irrigation method practically defunct in recent years, the Taliban were believed to be using these underground tunnels throughout the country to facilitate the movement of weapons and fighters.

The elders begged for a solution, preferably one resulting in the karez's destruction. The patrol debrief quoted one of them as having said, "The veins are black. There is no life left."

Within hours of the patrol's return to their outpost, those who had been in direct contact with the package fell ill, exhibiting high fever, pulmonary failure, and a series of spiral-patterned chemical burns covering the skin. Quarantine procedures were initiated, resulting in a complete lockdown and the alerting of a secretive, multinational task force designated to investigate various chemical and biological threats. Mac and Andy had been with the task force for three years, rotating the world over in search of the greatest boogeymen in the War on Terror. However, their utter lack of success during that period bred a cycle of cynicism that was commonplace among many involved in the war.

"You think we're hitting something this time?" Mac asked.

"Another dry hole, literally and figuratively," Andy said.

"Come on, you saw the brief. Those kids are beyond fucked up."

"I'll give you that. But is this some new bioweapon? I doubt it. Unless these dirt-farmers got lucky—maybe all that digging in the roads and culverts turned up a discovery, some long-dormant bacteria."

"What, like anthrax?"

"Sure, but even that's a stretch."

Senior Sergeant Jakub Pawel, the group's Polish representative, interjected, "I really hate these giant fucking holes, man."

Looming below the group and extending out for kilometers ahead was their objective. A string of gaping chasms, approximately five meters in diameter and spaced out every hundred meters, formed a straight line to the base of the mountains. Built around the edge of each pit was a mound of dirt set a meter tall, which further distinguished the structures against a backdrop of arid, bronzed clay and dust. Mac could only liken their unnatural appearance to crop circles—it was as if some giant had pierced the earth with a needle and left track marks, a monument to some forgotten mistake. The moon's light failed to penetrate its forbidding atmosphere, yet the karez beckoned to Mac, to the child in him who wished to explore such oddities.

The pilot announced over the intercom, "Approaching LZ Alpha."

"You ready, Andy?" Mac said while drumming on his knees.

"Absolutely."

The Blackhawk touched down about a kilometer from the end of the karez system. Andy, Senior Sergeant Pawel, and three others disembarked into a cloud of dust tinged with the scent of corroded metals and sulfur. Mac and the rest of the team would proceed further along the tunnel, inserting near the base of the mountain. Mac flashed a playful thumbs-down and a look of exaggerated horror from the helicopter as it set off for LZ Bravo. Andy responded with a smile and a salute, bringing only his middle finger to the tip of his brow.

Andy hailed the helicopter over his radio. "Haley Two-Four, this is Specter Two, over."

"Go for Haley Two-Four."

"In place at Site Alpha. Readings at the entrance are negative for chemical and biological traces. Preparing for descent. Over."

Beholder 56 - 20,000 Feet AGL
Sharana District, Paktika Province, Afghanistan
15 APR 2011 - 1526Z

"So, Rebecca—do you mind if I call you Becky? Anyway, how's that long-distance thing going for you and what's-his-name?"

"It's fine, Sir. We talk pretty much every day, so long as there isn't a comms blackout."

"What about marriage? You're doing that in the church, right?"

"Honestly, we haven't thought that far out, Sir. We're just trying to get this deployment over with."

"The Lord doesn't wait on our deployments. We can't be waiting on Him."

Jesus Christ, what a veritable fucking dinosaur. Captain Langstrom shifted in her seat and stared out into the darkness beyond the cockpit window of her turboprop aircraft. It didn't help. Today was Brigadier General Herzing's once-monthly excuse to truly experience the war by "logging some flight hours," and Langstrom had pulled the short straw again as copilot. The two senior airmen monitoring the equipment back in the cabin were, understandably, not in the mood to chitchat. Her "office" felt smaller than usual, no doubt due partly to the fact that General Herzing carried a few more pounds than the average pilot. *Just a few more hours chasing our tails, we land this bitch, and it's over.*

General Herzing straightened in his seat, then slouched his protruding gut forward. "I still can't get over the operation I supported last month. We tailed that Taliban on his bike for what, twenty minutes? Just maintained absolute focus on that dirtbag until the A-10s arrived. I'm tellin' you, a higher calling placed me in this seat that day. Things could've gone much differently otherwise. Your generation doesn't appreciate the importance of this war. We're bringing real civilization to these people. Real *faith*. I heard some of them think the Russians never left. They don't know what to believe."

A voice wavered from the back, "Uh, Sir, we're not picking up anything on the video sensors. Too much obstruction."

"Well, why didn't you say that earlier, Airman?" General Herzing made some adjustments to the flight controls. "Let's see if we can't get below this cloud deck."

The Karez
15 APR 2011 - 1545Z

Mac's voice came in over the radio: "Specter Two, this is Specter Five. We're not seeing much here. No signs of recent activity. It's pretty cramped. Will be slow progress to our first phase line. Over."

Andy responded, "Roger, Specter Five. We're seeing the same thing here."

Inside the karez, Andy's bulky combat boots struggled to find stability as he navigated a path barely wider than his shoulders. His night optical device offered marginal relief to his squinting eyes, as there was little natural light to enhance in the tunnel. With each probing step, clouds of ultrafine moon dust whisked into the air, adding fuzz to the picture provided by his NODs and spurring coughs among the team. Andy joked to Senior Sergeant Pawel, who was directly behind him in the tunnel, "I bet the Taliban have a dust factory hidden away. They're just cranking it out and playing the long game."

Pawel responded between coughs, half-joking, "No doubt a secret passed on from father to son. Our lungs have grown weak under the indulgence of clean air. They know this and use it against us, even at their own expense."

Andy's foot bumped against something, summoning a rattle that choked off the conversation. With his rifle pointing ahead, he kneeled and cautiously brushed dirt away from the object, revealing an old musket. The stock was curved, ending in a slight upward flare. Intricate pearl and bone fragments, cut in shapes resembling clovers and diamonds, danced on the wood's surface. It was the remnant of a lesson the West had abandoned over a century before, instead opting to simplify, romanticize, and memorialize a conflict through colorful Victorian paintings and dull encyclopedic entries. In reality, the blood and dust of that era were far more muted, the motivations nuanced.

"Specter Five, this is Specter Two. Evidence of a weapons cache. Over."

"Specter Two, Specter Five. We've found some old supplies—uniforms and canteens. Really old. Likely Soviet, maybe earlier. Over."

Andy felt out of place in the karez, like a clot obstructing an arterial flow. "Something's fucky. It doesn't look like anyone's been here in decades. Over."

"You think the Afghans gave us bad intel?" Mac said.

"When have they not?"

There was a brief, uneasy silence.

"Found an old Russian sniper rifle—what are the odds I get it back through customs?" Mac said.

"Good fucking luck."

"Maybe I'll ask one of the SOF dudes to send it—hold up."

A low rumble ran beneath the length of the karez, followed by a grinding metallic screech.

Andy froze. *Shit, IED?* "Scan your fives and twenty-fives," he said reflexively.

One of his squadmates laughed under their breath. "I can barely see a single meter ahead of my face in this bitch."

Andy struggled to recognize Mac's voice as it reverberated over the radio. "... good over there?"

Andy turned around to face the others. "Yeah, we're up here, but you're coming in broken."

An attempted response from Mac produced only static. The rumbling continued, shaking dirt loose from the tunnel's walls and causing Andy to lose footing. The floor beneath him sifted away under the vibrations, revealing a smooth patchwork of glossy ivory. Looking up, he noticed a round object birthed from the wall ahead. It tumbled, spurred by the tunnel's convulsions, before settling into a roll toward him. Visual artifacts streaked Andy's NODs, concealing the anchor of his growing dread until it came to rest near his rifle. A skull, polished as bright as white ceramic, stared at Andy with two gleaming coins settled deep in the sockets.

More bones were ejected along the length of the tunnel, propelled by ash, fumes, and pulsing white-hot light. Andy flipped up his NODs to avoid being blinded by the searing flashes, only to be confronted by a disorienting haze. A blended scent of plant matter and human waste sputtered throughout the space, bringing tears to Andy's eyes and delivering a blow beneath his sternum. The tears gave way to hypnagogic delights, as if images recorded on transparent acetate film had split his optic nerves and hijacked his senses.

The karez bled away into warm spring. Sprawling fields of poppies extended toward a distant mountain range, the face of which ebbed with purple hues in the heat. A figure towered above the foreground, a man walking with purpose. Atop his head rested a wool *pakol*, flowered and distinguished. The being's flesh was sloughing off the bone, yet this decay did not interrupt his stride nor weaken his grip on the long scythe resting over an exposed shoulder blade. Andy couldn't help but think of the musket he had encountered earlier when he saw the ancient design of the tool's handle. The blade appeared to have a different origin, hollowed out and filled with elaborate stained glass. It was brilliant, albeit brittle and impractical. The lightest of traumas could seemingly undo the craftsmanship.

In the giant's wake, a series of discarded blades jutted upwards from the earth, having naturally slipped from the snath at some point in their lives. The first, made of solid iron, resembled a plow's blade more than a scythe's. Its impact on the field below blighted the soil—the poppies refused to take root in its presence. Further up the path rested a blade carved from an ornate chessboard. Game pieces littered the ground around it, their once bright colors eroded by wind, the rules that governed their use lost to dementia. Finally, a blade of white marble stood at the edge of Andy's vision. Far more sizeable than the others, it featured the carving of a hero commanding a chariot, led into battle by four wrathful horses. The relics competed for Andy's attention, pleading for it, raging impotently for his acknowledgment as a man and soldier amongst the fields.

Each step of the decaying man produced a rumble, shaking loose a few more bits of muscle and sinew from his skeletal frame. The poppies bloomed as he passed, revealing an eye at the center of each blood-red flower. Some were mature; they appeared clouded and stricken with a fatalistic droop. Many were young, bloodshot, and weeping. Each projected some measure of distrust, whether hidden behind playful mischief or direct and unblinking. The watchers turned to face Andy, meeting his gaze and questioning his purpose.

A new image unfurled across the field, that of a man in his dress uniform, his nation's flag silhouetting a fresh yet artificially grim facade. It was the photo taken with the express purpose of serving as Andy's memorial portrait, should it become necessary. The rack of ribbons on the man's chest spoke of a testament to time, experience, and recognition. All were individual concepts that failed to attain relevance in this place. The photo would be his legacy, a simple memento to adorn a gravesite, perhaps later a fireplace mantel, for a brief moment in time. Those at home would not know of the transactions behind the accolades or the expense that others abroad would pay to fulfill a recruiter's promises to *change the world*, *become a part of history*, and *find meaning*. Andy reached out to the portrait to claim it as his own. It tumbled from the sky, ending its journey in a smoking pit of refuse. Andy fell after it, diving into the embers. The smell of jet fuel and plastic bonded to his skin, imparting legacy's exquisite toxicity.

Hoarse screams joined the symphony of fumes and light that erupted from the karez, the mountains relaying their torment to the deaf ears of departed Empire.

Beholder 56 - 14,000 Feet AGL
Sharana District, Paktika Province, Afghanistan
15 APR 2011 - 1606Z

Captain Langstrom's focus was hard at work, fidgeting with dials and building an invisible partition in the cockpit, hoping her body language alone would persuade General Herzing to drop all needless conversation.

An excited mumble came in over the intercom: "Uh, Ma'am? One of the radios is picking up something. The manual says it's a frequency for distress calls, but no one's talking. They're transmitting in the blind."

Fuck, here we go. Langstrom grimaced, knowing they'd be wheels down later than anticipated.

General Herzing's ears perked up. "Where's it coming from, Airman?"

"Ghazni province, Sir."

"All right, here we go!" The general hastened to the flight controls.

Langstrom interjected, "Sir, we'll need clearance before we can head that way."

"Becky, I am the clearance," the general said. "We've got some boys in trouble down there, and I'm betting we're the only available eyes within fifty nautical miles, especially given this weather."

Langstrom held in a sigh. "Senior Airman Jackson, get the battlespace owner for Ghazni in chat and let them know what's going on."

Task Force Duke Tactical Operations Center
FOB Andar, Ghazni Province, Afghanistan
15 APR 2011 - 1610Z

Specialist Bailey reclined in a dusty office chair and ran through a checklist of things he wanted to accomplish during his shift. "Breakfast" was out of the way; a to-go tray with surf 'n' turf scraps and an empty near beer were stuffed into a half-pint wastebasket under his plywood desk. He had a homework assignment to complete for an English distance learning course. A nearby pile of hastily scribbled flash cards served as a panic-inducing reminder of the upcoming promotion board Bailey had been warned to prepare for. His unclassified monitor displayed a shopping site. Boredom was compelling him to purchase yet another watch not authorized for wear while in uniform.

A slight blink caught his eye on a separate monitor. Someone had sent him a message.

1611Z<BEHOLDER_56> Are you the analyst for Ghazni Province?

Bailey hesitated. "Come on, not tonight, man."

1612Z<TF_DUKE_OPS> Roger

1612Z<BEHOLDER_56> We picked up a distress signal in your AO. Currently en route. ETA approx 1625Z.

1612Z<TF_DUKE_OPS> Location?

1613Z<BEHOLDER_56> Standby

1615Z<BEHOLDER_56> Vicinity grid 42S VC 602 151

Bailey jotted down the military grid reference on a scrap of paper and scrambled across the TOC to the operations battle captain, Master Sergeant Smith.

Master Sergeant Smith sighed as he minimized his web browser, setting aside the current argument he was having with his wife back home. "What is it, Bailey?"

"Master Sarn't, one of our aircraft picked up a distress call near this grid."

The battle captain squinted between the paper and Bailey, expecting the junior soldier to let slip that he had made the whole thing up. Everyone had grown complacent due to the Taliban's winter withdrawal. The soldiers' unwillingness to shake their shared delusion wasn't apathy but a natural desire to retreat from this most unnatural state of living. Day-to-day life had become a blurred collection of events marked by exploitation and death, masquerading in the fineries of a baser human connection that home could never offer.

"Well, shit. All right, Bailey, you and I are going to start making some phone calls. Let's make sure none of our units are operating in that space. Call the Polish up as well." The battle captain shifted his attention to the Afghan Army radio operators, their presence in the TOC that of unwelcome guests. "We'll need to check with them. Moe! Moe, I got somethin' here for you."

Mohammad, the interpreter on shift, hobbled over to the battle captain's desk, each step the definition of exaggerated feebleness. "Yes, Sir."

The battle captain motioned toward the Afghans, an expression of paternal sternness overcoming his face. "This is important, Moe. Ask them if they have anyone operating in this area. Get me an answer soon; they could be in danger."

"Yes, Sir."

Bailey walked back to his desk to find another message.

1616Z<BEHOLDER_56> Any recent insurgent
    activity in this area we should know
    about?

1619Z<TF_DUKE_OPS> Standby

1620Z<TF_DUKE_OPS> Negative. One of our line units had a few wounded in action near Khashek village a few days ago. They were disposing of some unexploded ordnance. Minor injuries. I heard they've already recovered.

1620Z<BEHOLDER_56> Roger

Mohammad's hushed whispers to the Afghans filled the plywood structure. Bailey and the others didn't interact with the Afghans much. Language was a substantial barrier, but it paled in comparison to suspicion. Besides, it was easier to laugh at them this way. Their radio etiquette was lacking to the point of absurdity—little more than men screaming into a handset, a futile performance of mind-numbing exhaustion. Bailey had asked once what the most common callsign he heard them use translated to: "Flood." What a weak name. American callsigns like "Wolfpack," "Punisher," and "Legion" were simply more evocative. It had never occurred to him that a force of nature could command intense fear and respect. Mohammad fell silent. Bailey tuned out the Pashto shouting that followed.

"SAILAB, SAILAB, SAILAB! ... SAILAB, SAILAB, SAILAB! ... SAILAB, SAILAB, SAILAB!"

Beholder 56 - 14,000 Feet AGL - The Karez
15 APR 2011 - 1626Z

Senior Airman Jackson braced himself for an inevitable backlash and made an announcement in the aircraft, "Sir, uh, I think we have eyes on the target area."

"Either you do, or you don't, Airman! What's the problem?" General Herzing said.

"Sir, we can see through some breaks in the cloud deck, but the picture is distorted. I'm thinking it may be some sort of hardware issue. I'm working on it now."

The general gave Captain Langstrom a sideways glance. "Where do the recruiters find these kids nowadays? They can't perform even the most basic tasks."

Langstrom, seeing an opportunity, struggled to hide her intentions as she jumped out of her seat. "I don't know, Sir. Sounds like they need some leadership back there. I'll be back shortly." The young officer had heard similar complaints enough times to discern that the general's issue wasn't one of age or experience, but of class. She stepped into the cabin and again questioned the company that her rank demanded she keep.

General Herzing quipped as he prepared for yet another risky descent, "Nothing an old man can't fix."

The Karez
15 APR 2011 - 1530Z

The clean, brisk air outside the karez summoned Andy to half-consciousness. Blurred stars shone through the clouds; a giant among them caught his attention. Venus? He brought his fingers to swollen eyes, scraping grains out from near the tear ducts, loathsome gifts from the tunnel below. His lungs seized with the cold, heaving their contents across his chest and into the dirt. As the wetness dissipated from his sight, the resplendence above revealed itself.

An aircraft? Thank fuck.

Andy began to drift again, his neck muscles giving way, cheek resting on the powder. The fruits of his lungs blossomed at the reaches of his vision: blood, mucus, and seeds, their sprouting roots mirroring the structures of his small airways and burrowing into the earth.

Task Force Duke Tactical Operations Center
FOB Andar, Ghazni Province, Afghanistan
15 APR 2011 - 1631Z

A curt voice boomed out of the phone: "Negative. Bravo Company has no active patrols in that area."

"Roger, thank you much, Sarn't." Specialist Bailey was struggling to identify the source of the distress signal. There were no Afghan soldiers, no U.S. patrols, and no coalition partners operating anywhere near this supposed cry for help. Bailey wanted a cigarette. Maybe a real beer. He settled for a piece of gum and looked at the video feed provided by Beholder 56. Glimpses through the clouds introduced an infrared view of a karez system. The cold, black holes stood out against the desert floor. As he squinted at his computer screen, Bailey felt a creeping, inexplicable disgust. Another text message from the aircraft sought his attention.

```
1632Z<BEHOLDER_56> Are you able to
    see the feed? We're having technical
```

issues, can't see our feed in the
aircraft.

1632Z<TF_DUKE_OPS> Roger, I see a karez.
Some clouds. Can you scan out from
this location? I'll try to identify
personnel/equipment.

1633Z<BEHOLDER_56> Copy

Bailey was on the hunt. His bloodhound might have been
partially blinded, but its sense of smell remained more than
adequate. The other soldiers in the TOC, having already
lost their taste for this fleeting entertainment, returned to
a debate about the Kyrgyz women working at the FOB's
barbershop. Bailey fused with the live video, his mind forming
and countering a multitude of explanations for such an unusual
event. There was a sudden tug at the leash.

1639Z<TF_DUKE_OPS> Pause scan.

1639Z<BEHOLDER_56> Roger

1639Z<TF_DUKE_OPS> Zoom in.

1639Z<BEHOLDER_56> Roger

An opening to the karez was pulsing with light, threatening
to drown out the entire image and drawing Bailey closer to
his screen. Between the pulses, he glimpsed a bright white trail
extending a few meters out from the hole, ending in a radiating
spiral nearly equal in size to the chasm.

"What the *fuck* is that?"

A human figure lay sprawled out at the center of the gyre, unmoving. A horrid rejection spewed from the earth; the sight of the body stained Bailey's mind and snuffed his speech. With each pulse of light from the screen, grotesque abstractions supplanted his linear thoughts and overwhelmed his vision.

Disembodied insectoid limbs of varying shapes and sizes twitch and convulse against a void of pure white. They pile together, split apart, and swirl in a desperate attempt to grasp.

A trail of eyes protrudes from infrared noise, staring back at the watcher and extending out indefinitely.

The Ring Road lies pitted and beyond repair. Flaming wreckage and viscera line it. Massive vehicles ruptured like tin cans—each a monolith to a few, a passing thought to many.

Thousands of men huddle under bridges, nodding along to celebratory gunfire while the skin on their arms rots away to reveal black poison.

The vicarious vivisection held Bailey, a vexing vision venturing through the vestiges of those vilified enemies he witnessed vanish on so many virtuous occasions. Vanish under the cover of darkness, within the depths of a *wadi*, and among clouds of smoke and fire. Imperceptible visages basking in the vitality of violence, the varying consequences of which, lacking valor, corrupt values and spurn any sense of validity.

A ringing from across the room knocked on the walls of Bailey's mind. The soldier's survival instinct kicked in, severing this newfound connection and overriding his state of catatonia. Thick clouds had since obscured the video feed on his monitor.

Master Sergeant Smith looked uncharacteristically professional, standing at attention with a phone to his ear.

"Uh, no, Sir. We couldn't confirm any friendly forces in the area. ... Roger, we didn't see anything with the aircraft. ..." The battle captain side-eyed Bailey. "No problem, Sir. If anyone asks, 'nothing significant to report.'"

Bailey rubbed his eyes and blinked hard, his urgency dampened by self-doubt. *Did I fall asleep?* He looked at the chat from Beholder, realizing the time he had lost.

```
1645Z<BEHOLDER_56> Do you want us to
   remain on this target?

1647Z<BEHOLDER_56> Continue scans?

1650Z<BEHOLDER_56> Comms check.

1655Z<BEHOLDER_56>     Will     continue
   scanning   the   area   until   we   hear
   otherwise or until clouds push us out.
```

Master Sergeant Smith appeared at Bailey's side. "You can let them return to base, Bailey. There's obviously no one out there."

"Master Sarn't, I think I saw something. We should send a patrol out to verify."

The battle captain squatted so that he was at eye level. "There's obviously no one out there, Bailey."

Bailey paused.

"Besides, we reached out to everyone. We know they aren't ours, right?"

"Well... Roger, Master Sarn't."

"All right, then. Fuck 'em."

Bailey returned his attention to his monitor. He looked down at his palms, winced, and wiped them on his pants. They grew hot under the friction. *What's the point? What does it matter who they were or who they belonged to? What am I doing here?* Bailey stuck an unlit cigarette in his mouth and sent a final message to Beholder.

Beholder 56 - 12,000 Feet AGL - The Karez
15 APR 2011 - 1705Z

```
1705Z<TF_DUKE_OPS>    Confirmed    no
  friendlies in that area. Thank you for
  the support.
```

The notification pinged on Senior Airman Jackson's console, provoking a near-silent cheer. The general's tyranny would soon come to a fruitless conclusion.

"Captain Langstrom, they're reporting no friendlies operating in the area. They've cleared us to RTB," the airman said.

General Herzing deflated, an acknowledgment that the days of his youth had once again escaped his grasp. He kept his eyes forward as Captain Langstrom entered the cockpit.

"That's damn unfortunate, Becky. Finding some Americans down there sure would have looked good on your next eval."

"Yeah, that's too bad, Sir."

The night's events lay frayed in Langstrom's mind, a gray tapestry fraught with hesitant inconsistencies through which she imagined hands reaching for hers. They would be irrelevant by next week, displaced among the firefights, adrenaline, and general white noise that distinguished existence in this country.

Perhaps, with time, they would resurface—those hands, by then long scorned, clenching her hair in vengeful fists and ripping her from the present. Another memory with her family, with herself, lost to those hands.

Senior Airman Jackson signed off in the chat.

```
1708Z<BEHOLDER_56> Roger, Beholder 56
    off station at 1708Z.
```

Location Unknown
Date-Time Group Unknown

The air was stale, layered with the scents of open wounds and powdered bone. The red angel above blinked away beyond the clouds, retracting its offer to those unfortunate enough to have witnessed its brilliance. Within days, the snare would be reset. Well within a century, it would be forgotten altogether.

iii. Simulacra

We arrived for job training on an early September afternoon. The air along the U.S.-Mexico border was crisp and infused with the fragrance of desert brush, a welcome change from the wet clay of summer on the East Coast. Someone ordered us off the bus, and we filed into an auditorium for a brief introduction with our "green suiters" (enlisted Army instructors, as opposed to civilians employed by a defense contractor).

"Perception is Reality," one of the green suiters said. It was our first lesson. Those three words alone wrought an environment of self-regulation that any middle manager would kill for. If you wanted to be viewed as a soldier, you needed to act like one, look like one, think like one.

Consider this: You're in a leadership position, but your subordinates don't acknowledge you. Well, then, you aren't a leader, are you?

You appear a bit overweight while in uniform. You're not physically fit, are you?

You asked to see a doctor for what seems to be a legitimate leg injury. Therefore, you're a "malingering" sack of shit.

You're a "female soldier" who appears to spend too much time with the men. Ergo, you must be "morally casual."

For instructors who purported to teach analysis methods intended to cut through the fog of war, one would think such a phrase would be considered counterintuitive. It is an effective weapon, however. It's something that, when applied systemically at the institutional or societal level, leverages an insidious form of control. "Perception is Reality" is not a truth but a *simulacrum*. It serves to build the map of truth and guide the landscape of human behavior to meet it.

It is this concept upon which our justice system runs, not the more commonly echoed "innocent until proven guilty." It is the reason police are incentivized to throw a laundry list of (often dubious) charges at the accused. Police interrogations are conducted with a future jury's opinion in mind. Plea deals are preferred over thoughtful and just legal analysis. Bureaucracy is utilized to break the will.

Our political institutions are attached to a life support system called "Perception is Reality." Threats and scapegoats pump the chest of a carcass devoid of resilience. Its bloat is acknowledged by the majority and maintained by a privileged minority. God bless America, so long as she refills my coffers.

Our communities have bought into the concept, hand over debt-clenching fist. If you don't shop like your neighbor, will they love you all the same? A "perfected" community in this great nation rises above petty behaviors such as differentiating based on skin color, gender, or sexuality, yet aligns morally with corporate branding and marketeers.

We engage a medical system sold on this concept in a futile attempt to buy more time. The patient's needs are minimized to support prescription writing. Those with complex ailments are strung along indefinitely, milked to the last dollar. Doctors are some of our society's most valued professionals, as are lawyers and CEOs, and their time is money.

Wars are broadcast, witches burned, and rituals discarded with this concept.

There is little to be gained in warring against "reality," at least for now. We can only recognize it where it is applied, educate others regarding its existence, and operate within a system that has succumbed to the pull of this artificial lodestar.

Omertà

"We're just performing our due diligence," the police lieutenant said, motioning toward a shadow box on the wall, a beautifully arranged façade of memories, forever static against a backdrop of deep blue felt. "I can see that you're like us—you understand the importance of due diligence, right? Thanks for being understanding." He motioned for the other officers to continue their search and left the apartment.

"We're nothing like you fucking pigs," Randy said, slumping on the sofa. The remaining officers carried on with their work, oblivious to his protest.

"Shit, Katy, what are you doing all the way over on this side of town?" one of them said to another.

"Speak for yourself! Ain't shit going on this close to Christmas. About fell out of my vehicle when I heard the call come in." Her continued rifling through the kitchen cabinets could only be described as an elaborate bureaucratic pantomime. "Figured I'd show up while it was still interesting."

She concluded the performance by stuffing her thumbs into the upper portion of her plate carrier—a rookie cop's attempt at peacocking the comforts of authority.

Randy's one-bedroom home was the subject of a haphazard autopsy, precious internals strewn about and documented, its former life measured by vulgar speech unfit for the dead.

"Check out all this gear!" an officer said. They had stripped the sheets from Randy's bed. In their place, the cops had dumped out old duffel bags, their contents staining the mattress with moon dust. Sun-bleached uniforms, packets of expired combat gauze, a few pairs of well-worn gloves, and a multi-tool had been staged and photographed next to a rifle.

"A lot of it's the same shit we're issued. Crazy," the female officer said.

No shit, city cop.

Randy stood up and wandered around the space, his hands clasped against his tailbone, assessing the damage. A moisture crack in the bathroom ceiling had been ripped open, exposing a hole large enough to fit Randy's head.

Huh. Looking for drugs?

The front door's handle had neatly imprinted on the adjoining wall during entry.

...and they'll expect me to pay for this.

He dismissed the thoughts with a flash of a frown.

"Hey, *you*, what the hell is this?" Officer Cox said. He raised an object in his outstretched hand, its silver sheen reflecting the cop's childlike anticipation.

"That's a kitchen scale," Randy said.

"Yeah, and what do you use it for?"

"To weigh my pet."

"Hmph," Cox said, discarding the scale and retrieving another object. His eyes twinkled. "And what about this?"

"That's a bag of peat moss."

"What's it used for?"

"It's bedding for my pet."

Cox dropped the bag on the floor, his shoulders drooping. The man's ginger-colored "special operator" beard was longer than Randy remembered. Something was off about his height as well; he stood barely a meter tall.

"Were you a medic?" an officer said from Randy's periphery.

"No," Randy said, annoyed that the fresh-faced kid had interrupted his musings. He looked the young twenty-something over, expressionless. There was a weight behind this one's eyes, a certain lightness in his chest. He had something the others didn't. Inexplicable.

He reminds me of myself... from back then.

"I wasn't going to tear into these, but we haven't found everything we're looking for," Cox said while walking toward a pile of neatly wrapped presents.

"I'm not watching this shit again," Randy said as he bounded across the living room, stepping through a recliner and intercepting Cox's path. With a heavy fist, he laid into the left side of the man's face. Cox stumbled backward and began to scream, his pitch oscillating with an artificial certainty that tickled Randy's inner ear. The row subsided as the cop came to rest on the carpet, triggering a standstill in the apartment. Sunlight dimmed. Randy studied the motionless body, its form draped in a veil of blurred pixels, visage obscured by pink and red noise.

A feminine, monotone voice filled the room. "You didn't choose violence back then. Why do so now?"

"Not a fan of this one, Doctor," Randy said as he stretched out on the sofa, his fingers searching for a texture in its fibers that was lost to them. He'd forgotten her name, this therapist, and was now too ashamed to ask.

"You mean Officer Cox?"

"No, I mean this memory. What the hell did you do to him, anyway? Sure, he had a Napoleon thing going on, but he wasn't a member of the goddamn Lollipop Guild."

"Studies show that veterans seek humor in dealing with stressors, especially those that overlap with their combat experiences."

"Yeah, where have I heard that before... Was that your attempt at a dick joke? For my sake? Doc, you shouldn't have."

"What's one lesson you've taken from this event—the arrest and subsequent search of your home?"

Randy closed his eyes. "A concealed handgun permit can and will be used against you as evidence of having committed a firearm-related crime, especially when they can't find much else."

"Let me rephrase: What have you come to learn about your behavior and its consequences?"

"Honestly, not much. Look, can we get to the part where I revisit my second deployment? There's someone I'd like to see."

"We could, but it's important that we review how the traumas of your time in the military have manifested in the years since. Acknowledging the role of consequence is a crucial step in the healing process."

"Come on, Doc. I really don't want to do this right now." Randy jutted his lower jaw forward, holding it in place narrowly beyond the threshold of discomfort.

The light bathing Randy's eyelids intensified; his words had reached God's ears. His thumb traced along a jawline textured with stubble and dried sweat. He smiled and opened his eyes, only to squeeze them shut when confronted by an intense glare reflecting off the thick gravel chunks beneath him. The COP's staging area revealed itself through short bursts of squint—sounds and smells of running diesel engines materialized at the sight of a vehicle column.

"Fuck yeah," Randy said, sitting upright and patting down the ammo pouches on his chest. His hand stopped at the leftmost pocket and reached in to retrieve a can of dip. He blinked through a tear while taking in its green tin, a shimmer that alone triggered his brain's pleasure centers.

"INCOMING! INCOMING! INCOMING!"

The squawk of an indirect fire alarm jolted Randy to his feet. *I didn't miss this shit.*

"Hey crackhead, get over here!" a voice called out from a nearby cement bunker, a six-foot-tall, squared tube that doubled as the platoon smoke pit.

"MOVING!" Randy heard the reply leave his lips and questioned his reflexive need to speak it within the ersatz.

"The fuck's taking you so long, soldier?" Staff Sergeant Diaz said from the bunker's entrance as Randy approached at a full sprint.

Randy felt a hand grab his shoulder that clumsily redirected his momentum further along the bunker's interior, causing him to stagger face-first onto a bed of cigarette butts and crushed plastic bottles. He recovered and dusted himself off, flicking tarred filters out of the webbing on his vest. "They even got the cheap knockoffs right," Randy said, holding one up for inspection.

"You sure like to keep us waiting, huh?"

Randy dropped the digital object upon hearing Kenny's voice. "You know me, gotta give Sergeant Diaz a good enough reason to be a dick, know'm sayin'?" Randy said as he clapped Kenny on the shoulder.

"What do you mean?" Kenny said, his head slightly tilted. *Still not him.*

Randy closed his stance. "How're things going with the wife, man?" he said. This conversation would have to do for now.

Outside the bunker, an eruption of shrapnel collapsed the platoon's favorite plywood shitter. Randy's ears failed to register the detonation, save for the bits of steel and rock that rained down against the concrete.

"That's a one-oh-seven!" Staff Sergeant Diaz said. "Stay the fuck inside!"

"Oh, you know. We're living the dream," Kenny said, unblinking.

"No. No, I don't," Randy muttered.

With a trailing scream, the last of the enemy rockets careened over the COP, crashing into a field several hundred meters away and fizzling out.

"Get some motherfuckin' accountability!" Staff Sergeant Diaz said.

Randy joined Kenny, who was peering from the edge of the bunker toward the rocket's point of impact near the shitters. Pungent smoke mingled with the smell of exposed human waste—a familiar, almost inviting acquaintance that Randy sought to shun. Outside, soldiers from Second Platoon clamored across the gravel, boots crunching in unison as they struggled to maintain their balance under the weight of a stretcher.

"Is that Bragg?" Randy said, craning his neck over Kenny's helmet.

A blanket of pixels enveloped the stretcher, their vague shapes permitting the interpretation that the mass below was human, albeit lacking a lower appendage.

"Yeah, must be Bragg," Randy said. He placed his hand on Kenny's shoulder, exerting a gentle pull that he recognized as self-serving yet disregarded in the face of an old addiction. "So, Kenny—"

A tender chime, followed by a slow flickering of the sun, dulled Randy's smile.

"That's all the time we have for today," the doctor said. "Please contact the scheduler for your next follow-up appointment."

"All right," Randy said. "Could we maybe—"

"Goodbye."

Randy's vision went black, then brightened again with the shapes of five hollow stars.

"We value your feedback," came a voice softened by a calm southern drawl. "Could you kindly share your rating for today's session? RTC, an AmmoDyne company, thanks you for your service to our great nation."

"Goddammit!" Randy said, tearing at his government-furnished VR headset and casting it aside. He looked at his watch. "Not even a full hour! Forty-five minutes every damn time! 'How're you doing? Do you want to try another medication? Do you have access to firearms? Uncle Sam wants me to ask if you feel like killing yourself today.'" Dry, cracked hands patted down pockets, hunting for a cigarette. "Are you even human? I'm doing just swell, doctor. I'm mighty fuckin' fine!"

♫ They give you a
hundred dollars and
take back ninety-nine. ♫

Randy's fingers welcomed a tingling numbness as they swept across aluminum and glass. His phone had, in fact, not been lifted while he was out. A cracked thumbnail jabbed at the screen's surface, launching a personal banking app. The monthly disability compensation check had landed in his account the day prior.

"I'll figure this out myself."

Randy was squatting in the middle of the aisle, carefully studying the purported answer to his needs and desires: The NineRealities Virtual Environment System. It was encased in a clean white box and perched behind plexiglass, a sterile arrangement masking an inherently volatile and messy premise. His eyes scanned back and forth between the box's product description and the price tag. The knots in his stomach demanded he continue pacing the store.

I can do a lot with fifteen hundred dollars.

He noticed an employee at standoff distance, a young woman studying his intent, her hands balled together and resting beneath her navel.

Randy sprang to his feet. "Hey! Uh, so I'm thinking about buying this," he said, trying to relax his smile for fear of appearing insane.

"The new headset? Sure, I can help you with that," the employee said, her checkered sneakers squeaking against the floor as she approached.

Randy squinted at her nametag. "Uh, hi, LeAnna. Does this thing do everything they say it does?"

"Well, I've never tried it myself, but I believe so," she said, her eyes fixed on the shelf. "They say you don't need to buy games anymore. This creates it all on the spot—knows what you want to see." Her eyes shifted to meet Randy's, flashing concern. "You know they require a subscription for this?"

"What doesn't these days?" Randy said with a laugh. "Everything's rent. I figure it's cheaper than therapy—I mean, the government pays for mine. It's not all that great, though. Get what you pay for, right?"

"Yeah... If you're sure, I'll go ahead and bring this to the register for you."

Randy's head gave a slight, visible shake. "Yeah. Yeah, let's do it."

Randy shuffled behind LeAnna, dreading the stare of each customer he passed on his way to the front of the store. He looked down, acknowledging the sorry state of his appearance. Stale and soiled—a time capsule of fashion harkening back to a boy who existed before the service. At least in this regard, he was much the same as he'd always been.

Jesus. You look ate-the-fuck-up today.

Once at the register, Randy handed over his ID and debit card, keeping his eyes downcast.

"Oh, I can give you a veteran's discount."

"I appreciate it." Randy managed a brief nod.

Randy saw LeAnna's smile for the first time as the payment cleared.

"Be careful how you use this, okay? There's some weird stuff out there," she said.

"I'm not meeting with anyone else. Single-player." Randy returned an awkward smile.

"I'm just saying, as someone who spends too much time on the internet, there is a lot of fringe counterculture that seems... I dunno, not organic?"

"How do you mean?"

"Like, I wouldn't be surprised if the government sponsors or creates content specifically to monitor how we engage with certain ideas."

"What, like political ideas? Anarchism?"

"Think smaller, much smaller than that. Who shows interest in using psychedelic drugs to communicate with the dead? What portion of the population is most likely to fall victim to a financial dominatrix? What does the journey to society's edge look like?"

"You're saying they're mapping the underbelly?"

Those who can't or won't participate along with everyone else.

"Exactly. Like a running census. That's my tin-foil hat theory, anyway."

"Got it," Randy said, his voice warming to the interaction. "Don't let the intrusive thoughts win."

"Wait here. I'll be right back."

Oh shit. Was this a test?

She's gone to call the cops. Maybe she's connected to a government agency?

She returned with a bottle of water and a corporate-branded T-shirt. "These were taking up space in the breakroom; you should have them."

"Oh. Thanks."

Evening settled over the living quarters—what passed for them, anyway. Plywood, dust, cots, more dust, rat shit, and privacy curtains strung along with 550 cord. Randy took in the sight of the structures, illuminated by a full moon and a clear, starry sky, a vision he thought he'd never again behold. No streetlights washing out the night, nor pavement holding in the heat. He walked toward the Scout Platoon quarters, a shelter among shelters, its doorway open and obstructed by Staff Sergeant Diaz, who was busy hazing a junior soldier.

"Why are you so jacked up, soldier?" Staff Sergeant Diaz said, his arms crossed, pelvis extended forward. "You don't fix this shit, and I'm sticking your ass on permanent tower guard, know'm sayin'?"

Randy transitioned his walk to a goose step, halting at the threshold to render a dopey salute.

"The fuck you lookin' at, dick-suck?" Staff Sergeant Diaz said, his whole hand now outstretched and pointed at Randy's chest.

"Ah, yes, good day to you, sir!" Randy said with an exaggerated bow. A tourist in his own domain, Randy sought to test the social contract that governed it, dismissing its blemishes with absurdity.

"Sir? Hey, shit-dick, I work for a living—"

"I said good day!"

Staff Sergeant Diaz doubled over, his nose touching his shins. His body proceeded to fold upon itself repeatedly until Randy lost sight of it in the dirt.

"An appropriate end for a cartoon villain," Randy said to Diaz's recent victim. The young soldier continued beating his chest against the ground, unaware of Randy's presence.

Randy strolled in, guided by the sweet perfume of memory to his old cot, its grease-stained nylon hidden under an even greasier lightweight sleeping bag. Kenny was sitting on the cot next to it, reading a letter.

"Your mom still crying about you being over here?" Randy said, giving Kenny's shoulder a playful shake.

"It's my wife this time," Kenny said. "Complaining about how my paychecks aren't enough. I don't think they got the baby added as a dependent yet."

"Sounds like it's high time we take a trip to the FOB and put a boot up the admin clerk's ass, know'm sayin'?" Randy said with a grin of anticipation.

Kenny tossed the letter aside, leaping at Randy and throwing weightless punches into his stomach. "I. Told. You. Don't. Say. That. SHIT!" Kenny said between blows, a restrained smile forming. "You know how much I hate Diaz."

It's you. It's finally you.

Randy fell back onto his cot, tears forming in his eyes. "How've you been, man?"

"Good, I suppose. Five months, fifteen days, and...," Kenny checked his watch, "ten hours left."

"Yeah, well. Show me a picture of that kid of yours again."

"Sure," Kenny said, retrieving a photo from between the pages of a nearby book and handing it to Randy. "She said he's quite the little shit." He pulled a can of dip out of the pocket near his ankle, gave it a few flicks, and set a pinch of tobacco against his gumline. "Just like me."

"Yeah, man. I wonder how the little dude is doing now."

Maybe I should give him a call.

"He might like to hear from you," Kenny said. "Tell him the stories I won't."

"I might have to do that. Hey, you remember that mortar that landed not too far—"

A deafening crash hammered Randy's ears. He ducked and squeezed his eyes shut. Silence. He fought against his hesitation, opting instead for weak confrontation. The Scout Platoon dwelling ceased to be, replaced by the internals of the old communications building, its plain concrete walls marred by bullets and ball bearings.

Oh, no. No, no, no.

No!

Randy exited the simulation. It was dark outside. He pulled a blanket over his curled body and began the hunt for sleep.

It knows what you want to see.

The headset was always within arm's reach, yet it had spent the last three days under a heavy wool blanket, its bonds not yet set, expectations unrealized. Instead, Randy chose the company of a bottle and a near-constant stream of online personalities whose words scraped along the surface of his brain with a dull, numbing relentlessness.

It knows what you want to see.

The cream-colored plastic felt soft to the touch—foreign, an affront to fragile identities, like silk against the skin of the peasant. A connection that should not be. Hands unworthy. A mind too poor to appreciate such potential, to grasp at heights beyond affording.

What do you want to show me?

"EOD folks reported they swept the building for unexploded ordnance last night," Kenny said. "Five dead dudes in suicide vests, some RPGs, a few grenades. Wasn't much left after everything that happened... lookin' like the goddamn O.K. Corral in here."

Not this. Not again.

The morning prior, insurgents had stormed the provincial communications building, halting its broadcasts proclaiming the legitimacy of the U.S.-backed central government. What followed was a ten-hour firefight, a grueling standoff hailed as a major accomplishment and a turning point for Randy's battalion. The unit's leadership would later reminisce about the sight of Second Platoon peeling away at the building's exterior and of the sound of the Apache's autocannon strafing the roof, of the sniper teams hammering the windows and of the insurgents bundled under mounds of prayer rugs, cowering under a might so raw and righteous as to crumble the structure around them. "God wills it!" they would jest, irony incarnate.

The fighting ended only after local commandos stormed in through an exterior stairwell. Two of the insurgents clacked off, detonating vests packed with explosives and steel scrap—the others were shot dead before the opportunity to commit self-martyrdom presented itself.

With the sun rising on a new day, Scout Platoon had been tasked with collecting forensic evidence from the scene. Staff Sergeant Diaz had assigned Randy and Kenny to a corner office, an awkwardly placed room at the end of an offshoot from the main hall.

"Why the fuck was the building not secured overnight?" Randy muttered to himself.

"I'd bet that EOD lieutenant got to complaining about the cold. Can't blame her. A sleepover with a bunch of dead guys and a handful of assholes like us—sounds legit," Kenny said, shaking his head. "They turned security over to the police, who I'm sure were lured off by boredom and *hashish*."

Randy kicked at a loose chunk of concrete.

No one had a clue who was coming and going after those clowns left.

"That's why they sent us. Never a dirty ass we won't wipe," Kenny said, retrieving a digital camera from his pack and snapping pictures. Spent shell casings and shattered glass littered the floor, reflecting wisps of sunlight onto the ceiling.

"Fuck that."

I was ready to end it at this point.

"Me too, man. But don't let Diaz hear that—he'll drive the bus right over you, repeatedly," Kenny said.

"How about we just drop this shit and have a smoke out by the vehicles?"

"We don't have a choice," Kenny said, raising his camera toward the corner of the room. "What the hell is that?"

Randy knew the answer: stacks of thick rugs, powdered with dirt and calcium, crushed under a large section of the collapsed ceiling, a lifeless hand reaching from beneath. The image had thrived in his mind's recesses, decades burrowed, ready to surface at the slightest pressure, its concealed rationality and continued existence indebted to the fact that no one is ever at the wheel, that the intangible is blameless.

Kenny reached for his radio. "Tyrant Six, Tyrant Three-Three, over."

The radio crackled: "Go for Tyrant Six."

"EOD cleared the building of suicide vests, correct?" Kenny said.

"Roger."

"I think they missed one."

"Unlikely. Check it out and report back. Out."

Randy reached for Kenny's arm. "Let someone else handle this," he said.

This thing's not working.

His hand passed through Kenny, who continued toward the body.

"You know Diaz will kill us if we don't do our due diligence," Kenny said.

"Dammit, it's not a vest!"

Kenny squatted at the edge of the rugs, no longer responsive to Randy's thoughts.

Not again. Please!

Randy shut his eyes as Kenny located the bottommost layer of dyed wool and lifted.

Click.

The click.

Where's the click? I can't run without the click. How will I know to move if there's no click? Without the click, it's still there. It's still waiting, waiting for him. He won't shove me out the doorway without it. If there's no click, he's not dead yet. It's holding me here. Again. Every time. I live here—live in this. I'm so tired.

Randy kneeled beside Kenny, a witness. Kenny's eyes were vacant, disembodied, the way they are at first sight of the dead. The body was crushed beneath the waist, the explosive vest still intact.

But... they said they cleared the building... said it was a trap set by the insurgents after the police left, right? RIGHT?

♫ *Your left, your left,*
your left, right? ♫

Everyone said that. The report said that. His wife was told that. His son knows that. It was a trap, cowardly, like they do, like they are.

Now you show me this?

Why are you gone? Because someone couldn't do her job? No!
It should have been me. I have no one.

What do I do with this? Find the bitch responsible? Make her pay?

She fucked up and your death was because of her fuckup and by now she's had a career and a life and no one even thought about whether your life was more important!

TELL ME! WHAT DO YOU WANT ME TO DO?

Randy awoke to a steady stream of water droplets against his cheek—a warm summer rain. The cardboard that patched the gap in the driver's-side window had come loose again. He removed his headset and fumbled around the cupholders for another pill.

You turn against me one more time, and we go straight to the pawnshop. No more chances.

There was a slight grainy texture to the sky, like old film artifacts embedded for the sole purpose of communicating the feeling that things should be better now, but they aren't. Kenny's lone form was a blip on the ridge ahead. Beyond him, a small village, appearing vacant, shook under the repeated buzzing of a pair of fighter aircraft. Looping, diving, ascending. Randy floated over to Kenny, and the two sat along the crest, their legs dangling over a near oblivion.

Randy found his center, a lit cigarette. "We shouldn't be sitting like this. We're silhouetted against the sky; they'll see us."

"We're safe here. Always have been."

"It sure doesn't feel like it. It never feels like it."

"What are you doing when this is over?" Kenny said.

"Back to mourning, I guess."

"It's been a while. You should find something else worthy of your time."

"They took my forty days, Kenny. I never saw your body—couldn't attend the funeral. I resigned myself to grinding away in this shithole until they said we could go home. Now that I'm back, I can't stop, shouldn't stop, not for you."

"How old is my son?"

"Oh, he's gotta be in his thirties by now."

"And how many times have you seen him?"

"Never. I don't know if I can."

"You're spending your time with the wrong version of me. He needs to know what only you can tell him."

"What? The truth? That you died for a mistake, a mistake that was written off so an officer could protect their career? You know what I'll see in your son, right? The gift of the ghost, a man holding all my memories and none of yours. He doesn't deserve my misplaced anticipation, my hesitant hopes, my association with his old man."

"What do you mean by that? I wouldn't have anyone else speak for me."

"I live out of my fucking car, Kenny, and I can barely manage that."

Kenny turned to meet Randy's gaze. "I don't mean to sound like an asshole, but you're all jacked up. It pains me to see it."

"I finally had a chance to visit your grave after I got out. Section Sixty. Another funeral was going on that day, somewhere out among Arlington's recent expansions. I heard the guns echo off the hill where the rose gardens mark two hundred years. I've rejected that salute every day since, rejected the salute of twenty guns while seeking the favor of one."

"And yet here you are, still rucking, even if it's just block by block, city to city. I can see you're holding out for something, something more than this farce."

"It should be you in here, talking to my ghost. At least you'd have family on the outside, someone to come back to, less to escape from. Better yet, we should have never been there. We were kids, Kenny. I'd rather you lived and… and we just separated after the service, lost touch. I think I'd rather have gone the rest of my life wondering where you ended up, what your career was like, if you were just as lonely as I was. Alone but linked, linked by this place, a fever dream. I can't live with uncertainty; it's my greatest fear. But I'd take a lifetime of that over this."

"I'd like to think it was all for something," Kenny said, placing a weightless hand on Randy's shoulder. "Dying, I mean. My boy pulled through, became stronger because of it. My absence produced a standard—*the* standard—for what to accomplish, how to live. Better than a man who was real and riddled with the faults and burdens I collected here."

"Don't say that!" Randy said, sobbing.

"I'm not even who I was, Randy, only your reflection of me. I think it's time you find what you're living for while you still can."

No, I won't believe that! You are him! Just as I remember, as I've always remembered!

I need to go. I need to go home. I need to leave. Someone is waiting for me. There's someone I need to see.

…Who is it?

Who is IT?

"Goddammit, WHO IS IT?!"

"Mr. Randy, sugar, you're having a bad dream again." A familiar voice, a hand pressed firm against the chest, the return of light as the headset was removed.

Randy's eyes went wide; he gasped after a slight apnea.

"It's Ms. LeAnna. You're safe, sugar." She dabbed at Randy's mouth with a washcloth. It smelled of laundry, with a subtle hint of the unclean, sour. She turned to the young nursing assistant at her side. "He was probably visiting his friend, Mr. Kenny. He lost him in the war. Sometimes, he just needs a break."

"Is this really safe? For *them*? For us?" the woman said.

"You don't understand. He wants it. I can't keep him out of the helmet for more than a few hours without starting a fight. Isn't that right, Mr. Randy?"

Randy brought his fingers to his lips. They were parched, curled inward, and stubbled white. "LeAnna? When were you promoted? I knew you were too good for the electronics department."

"Why, thank you, Mr. Randy," she said, bringing her hands to her hips, a playful gesture.

"How did you get here—in this country? Did you bring your passport? You should be careful; I think they're setting up on the ridge again. It's been too long since the last rocket attack."

LeAnna guided a straw to his mouth. "From cradle to grave, we need these screens, always these screens. We crave them, crave the comfort."

Randy's hand gripped the bedsheets and twisted.

"Here we go, Mr. Randy," LeAnna said, placing the headset over his eyes. "Say hi to Mr. Kenny for me."

iv. Defeating the Narrative: "Seeing Combat"

Who is allowed to experience the consequences of military service?

"Fewer than fifteen percent of enlisted personnel ever see combat or are assigned a combat role."

This convenient little factoid eases the burden for the military recruiter, assuaging the fears of every parent reluctant to support their child in "signing the dotted line" for Uncle Sam, while obscuring the full range of hazards associated with military service. It's similarly parroted in public forums, by veterans unable or unwilling to compromise the nature of their trauma-based identities, by useful idiots targeting the socialized structure of the veteran disabilities compensation system, or by artificial entities drumming up support for continued empire-building.

Is participating in physical combat with other humans the exclusive gateway to experiencing physical, emotional, and moral injury as they relate to military service? One could argue that the very act of enlistment dramatically increases one's proximity to a complex culture of violence, as well as its inherently negligent, dangerous, and varied subcultures.

Some scenarios:

You're a radio operator in a tactical operations center, relaying the communications of soldiers engaging enemy forces. Your purpose is explicitly defined—a crucial link between the "boots on the ground" and higher headquarters. One day, a voice stricken with panic spills over the radio waves. He cries out in bouts of unintelligible fear. You try to help, but without a location, callsign, or understanding of the situation, there's little you can do. The pressure is overwhelming.

As an aviation survival equipment specialist, you've been selected and qualified to load nuclear munitions onto aircraft. The drills you regularly perform are just training, of course, although you can't help but think that one day they won't be. How many lives will be taken?

You're a young woman of color who has recently been assigned to the logistics office at your first unit. Your coworkers—two young women and a male supervisor nearly twice your age—are of the same race. The supervisor is somewhat overprotective, but he seems to mean well and teaches you everything there is to know about your job. As time goes on, however, his behavior morphs into that of a mother hen. He begins questioning your activities outside the office, reminding you that you have an image to uphold. If a man of another race enters the office and speaks with you or your coworkers, whether for business or otherwise, your supervisor becomes irate, launching into an expletive-laced rant the moment you're alone with him. This behavior escalates to the point where you feel his possessive gaze on you at all times, even outside of the work environment.

You're a petroleum supply specialist on your second deployment. With little to do in your traditional role, you're assigned to permanent tower guard duty. After a few weeks of uneventful shifts staring into the desert beyond the base perimeter, you decide enough is enough. You commit to a classic deployment mantra, a list of priorities for your time outside the tower: Get Jacked, Get Tanned, and Do Laundry.

You start hitting one of the base gyms, affectionately referred to as "the prison gym." There, you meet some like-minded individuals who introduce you to the ease of accessing the European steroid market—click, ship, juice. Your time in the "sandbox" drags, and you begin chasing other highs to escape the monotony. One day, the sergeant responsible for getting soldiers to and from their shifts in the towers finds you face down in bed, rigid, with a can of compressed air held to your mouth.

You're a young woman who has recently returned from a deployment to Iraq. You are reunited with your husband, who has since followed you into military service. You become pregnant. Your husband strangles you and leads investigators to believe that your cause of death is related to your injuries sustained in Iraq. He claims the proceeds of your life insurance policy, using the funds to establish a domestic terror group within his unit. He orders the killings of two others before his crimes are exposed.

During your military career, you've been sent to locations spanning the globe: Hawaii, Kuwait, Afghanistan, and Vietnam, among others. Unfortunately, your body has no choice but to remind you of these experiences. Toxic open-air burn pits, tap water resources tinged with jet fuel, and DNA-altering industrial chemicals have left you and your comrades with respiratory diseases, cancers, and other severe challenges to daily living. Every environmental incident dragged into the light represents a complex legal battle for acknowledgment and compensation. And yet, the pattern persists.

As a young woman and trained small-arms and artillery repairer, you're assigned to a base along the U.S.-Mexico border. You are sexually harassed, assaulted, and brutally murdered. A legitimate investigation is conducted months later, only after being prompted by mass protests.

You're a soldier serving in a non-combat role in your unit's headquarters building. One of the offices down the hall receives a new transfer, a crusty sergeant from the military police. You're not sure why he's here now, but he's funny. He's got a habit of cracking jokes that safely test socially acceptable thresholds without becoming outright inappropriate. A few months pass, and he disappears unexpectedly from the office. You learn that he's been arrested by civilian authorities and charged with possession of child pornography. Was your unit's commander onto something when they transferred him away from his duties as a military police officer? You shrug and try not to think about it.

You're a veteran in the middle of appealing to the Department of Veterans Affairs for disability compensation benefits. You were sexually assaulted during your military service and have sustained lifelong mental injuries as a result. You access the Board of Veterans' Appeals database—a server containing many thousands of veteran disability cases that were initially denied and brought before a judge for adjudication—and search for the phrase "Military Sexual Trauma" (MST). The acronym feels both like an acknowledgment of your pain by the government and a bureaucratic insult. You pore over thousands of cases involving veterans who were subjected to the same violence, sustained physical and mental injuries, and required months or years of appeals for those injuries to be recognized.

You don't make much money as a newly minted, junior enlisted soldier. Personal finances are difficult enough, but they quickly become nightmarish once your husband leaves you alone to raise a baby. One of the senior enlisted soldiers, a certified advocate for your unit's sexual assault prevention program, hears about your difficulties and offers you a chance at a lucrative side hustle: prostitution.

Find any veteran, ask if they'd agree with a son's willingness to enlist, and you might receive mixed opinions.

Then, ask the same about a daughter.

Non-Combat Related Incident

War does not suffer cowards,
Nor brothers under the pressure of strife,
Nor furthermore, leaders in distress,
When Perception is Reality.

The soldier's reflection,
Skillfully crafted,
Seeks strength among the ranks;
For alone, it lacks resilience.

Broken down, built again,
Devotion is the bond;
Rejection below, ignorance above,
Stains the pride of the Cased Banner.

I shall sing now of Ed's Bane;
Liaison of Violence,
Bearer of Shame,
Messenger for the All-American.

Fortress of the South,
Alexandropolis,
Seat of the Pashtun;
Ed's Bane was sent.

Alone in bearing,
With blessings of the 82nd,
The Messenger sought
Guarantees of the High One.

The Two-Star received,
Ed's Bane and others;
In presence of the War Council,
Discussed plans for future raids.

Sound in approach,
Confident in speech,
Our Messenger delivered
Representation for Conflict.

The Beckoner of War,
Wisened of Battle,
Did ask of His Council,
Their intent to support.

"No word has been sent
Prior to this joining,"
Spake the Thunderer, King of Battle,
"But our guns are plenty."

"We are not so fortunate,"
Spake the Seasoned Wind-Rider.
"Our Fighters have been promised
To those more earnest in request."

Finally, the Broker of War-Ravens
Did speak to Ed's Bane,
"Our Eyes are averted,
For lack of your planning."

The High One proclaimed,
"I begrudgingly approve
Your ill-planned raid.
Convey my warning to your Commander."

Bitter Success
Did Ed's Bane return;
The Hollow Fang of Bureaucracy
Delivers Venom to the Messenger.

"Our raid is approved
With words of caution;
The War-Father demands
Greater skill in planning."

"Advice of the Career-Minded
I shall not heed,"
Spake the Warmonger,
Chief among the All-American.

"Any mistakes made
Are surely yours.
The words of the Messenger
Lack the strength of my will."

"Are you not an Officer?
Agent of Men?
My plans never lack,
Though I question your tenor."

The Messenger anguished,
Wading pools of darkness;
Ed's Bane sought vigor,
Once prided, now lost.

Doomed meetings of Council,
Bring further disappointment;
The Face of the Formation,
Bears the weight of incompetence.

Voices intrude,
Upon Ed's Bane's Seclusion;
Eroding taboos,
Making way, a new plan.

"Failed the men.
Failed yourself.
A father's namesake,
Collecting dust."

"Am I not a Soldier?
Have I not been proven?
The Land Between Two Rivers,
A bloody war, I witnessed ended."

"Even now,
An accomplishment in vain;
A New Dawn fades,
Beneath Legions of Black Banners."

"I must reclaim
A dominance tarnished;
I'll face the Council,
A final act, my decision awaits."

Early morning,
Saw Ed's Bane return;
The Fighting Season,
Had not yet sprung.

Before the High One,
Hostile demands were rendered;
False strength draped in Image,
Reveals silent desperation.

The War Council spake,
"Who is this man before us?
Of behavior abhorrent,
A reasonable request, dead without tact."

A young man rejected,
Leaves the High One's Hall;
Vision and Reflection shattered,
Amidst the War-Gathering's confusion.

The voices return,
Yet a hope flickers;
Waning resolve,
Bargains for a future.

A final visit,
Ed's Bane appeals,
The War Council's members,
Apologies and guarantees.

Ed's Bane was received
With kind hesitation;
Who knows a man's mind,
His dealings within?

With redress given,
The messenger returns to his bed;
A silence, calming,
An audience with the darkness.

With weapon in hand,
And opportunities fading,
Ed, Ed's Bane, answered the darkness,
Delivered himself unto the Void.

A discovery made
By partner in dwelling,
A sick man
Makes light, a brother's death.

War-Grief returns
To the High One's Hall;
The burden of hindsight
Splinters the mind.

The Banner of the All-American
Remains untarnished;
The Colors, cased,
And War's Ichor dares not touch them.

v. Delusions of a Warrior Caste

I am a third-generation U.S. military veteran and a fourth-generation contributor to the U.S. military-industrial complex. Ours is a legacy of involvement in the American business of war, one that began with the gestation of the atomic bomb and, if my efforts succeed, will be laid to rest with the advent of the so-called era of "Great Power Competition."

Some believe that an American "warrior caste" solidified during the GWOT Era. The idea seems plausible on paper. Pentagon reports from 2016 indicated that over 25% of new military recruits had a parent who also served in the U.S. military, while 80% came from families where at least one other member previously served. Additionally, as of 2022, veterans made up just 6% of the U.S. population, while active-duty service members comprised less than 1%. My family's legacy certainly appears to support this theory.

However, as is often the case with GWOT-Era narratives, data lacking careful interpretation and personal anecdotes without context result in significant knowledge gaps. The warrior caste narrative discards social and economic trends that drive military culture and recruitment while embracing the convenience of the simulacrum.

Let us consider:

The warrior caste narrative promotes the myth that all current and former military service members share a uniform set of values—values that the common American seemingly cannot appreciate or understand. It aspires to a reality in which these values are more closely aligned with those of romanticized and historically distorted warrior cultures than with those of the people our military is sworn to protect. In truth, both the values and motivations of service members are varied and nuanced. While economic incentives may not be the sole driver of military enlistment, they are at least as significant as factors like patriotism and legacy.[1]

Any caste formation resulting from the GWOT Era is more closely tied to political and economic factors than internalized identity. And, if such a caste did form, it was largely confined to the commissioned officer ranks of the military. Evidence of this can be seen in the members of the ruling class who used their military commissions as a springboard for careers in national politics, as well as in the hiring practices of tech, finance, and consulting firms. Attending one of our nation's war colleges offers an exclusive pathway through the revolving door between the Pentagon and its partners in private industry.

The warrior caste narrative is tainted by incentive. The DoD contributed to and directly benefited from its dissemination. Exclusivity drives group cohesion, as does proselytism and its consequent resistance. Similarly, market incentives cannot be discounted. The entertainment industry thrives on fantasies associated with warrior caste membership, while the merchant of the day hawks performative masculinity—T-shirts and bumper stickers communicate desires to align with the state and the violence inherent in its dominion.

A true American warrior caste is unlikely to take shape outside of political posturing and marketplace fantasies, a direct result of the GWOT and its consequences. The legacy families have been hollowed out. The goodwill meticulously cultivated following the disaster of Vietnam was discarded along the roadsides of Iraq and Afghanistan. Don't believe it? Look at the recruiting methods put to use since the end of the GWOT Era. First- and second-generation immigrants from Latin America are increasingly targeted for U.S. military recruitment. Spanish-language advertisements permeate television, radio, and social media. Cash incentives and paths to U.S. citizenship seek to patch the growing gaps in military recruitment no longer maintained by superficial rites of heritage.

For now, our political leaders are content with where they lay blame for poor enlistment numbers and the demise of a warrior caste that never existed: The majority of our children are simply too fat, medicated, and stupid to seek membership among the warrior elite.

Calls for conscription and mandated national service, naively dismissed as remote absurdities, continue to echo throughout the public forum. From where do they originate? Do the halls of our veterans truly ring in agreement?

---

1. To be clear, I do believe that economic incentives drive the majority of modern recruitment, while other, more patriotically aligned motivations are often cited to dissociate from the shame that accompanies economic hardship.

Waidmannsdank

A TRAGEDY IN THREE ACTS

<u>Dramatis Personae</u>

Bastian Bindewald: Grandfather, late 60s. A veteran, his identity is captured by the tangles of nostalgia.

Andreas Bindewald: Father, mid 40s. An active yet reluctant professional, torn between tradition and personal aversion.

Arthur Bindewald: Son, early 20s (Acts I and II) to mid 30s (Act III). The clean slate, subject to desires both informed and imposed.

The Third: The promoter. The inciter. The disconnected authority. A being without defined age or gender.

Anna: Audience member, late 20s.

Johannes: Audience member, early 40s.

Scene & Time

Act I: Duchy of Württemberg, 1525.

Act II: Iraq, 2006.

Act III: United States, Present Day.

ACT I

Scene 1

SETTING: *A forested region in the Duchy of Württemberg. A campfire burns outside a communal hunting cabin, surrounded by dense trees.*

AT RISE: *BASTIAN and ARTHUR are seated around the fire, huddled closely.*

ARTHUR

> *(ARTHUR yawns.)*

BASTIAN
It's too early to be yawning, my boy! And before breakfast, even!

ARTHUR
> *(rubbing eyes)*
Sorry, Opa. I didn't sleep well last night. Nightmares.

BASTIAN

What of?

(There is a pause.)

ARTHUR

I walked a path in darkness, archways looming overhead and draped in ribbons of fine silk. There were others, mostly stumbling, blank eyes. I was against the flow. They were like cattle blocking my intent—I applied force when my words failed to part them.

BASTIAN

Righteousness is not without its obstacles; you will come to know this.

ARTHUR

The path ended on a shore. To my left was a river, wide and inviting. To my right, a dwelling. My father was inside—at least, I think he was. I felt a presence I knew to be his, even in his long absence.

BASTIAN

Did you enter?

ARTHUR

No. I awoke to a crash. You didn't hear it?

BASTIAN

(BASTIAN stares, fixed yet unfocused, into the audience.)

My sleep was fleeting—a visit from old ghosts. I had naught
but their memories and the silence to converse with. The
anticipation of your first hunt is attempting to mire you. Do
not allow it.

(placing his arm around ARTHUR's huddled shoulders)
Show me your weapon. Is it ready?

ARTHUR

(stretching to retrieve a long rifle, which leans against a nearby
stump)
Of course, Opa. The bore is free of fouling, and the matchlock
shines in the early morning moonlight. I've done just as you
taught me.

BASTIAN

(inspecting the rifle)
I see! May it serve you as well as it served me.

ARTHUR

And what of your first hunt, Opa? Was it successful?

BASTIAN

Hm. I certainly lacked your discipline. They were different
times; the training was lacking. The swine were
overpopulated; they had uprooted towns and overrun the
Duke's forests to such an extent that even poor young men
like me were afforded the chance to enter his service.

ARTHUR

How many did you slay in those early days?

BASTIAN

(rubbing his chin and cheek)

That is a question the hunter never answers. We shall never boast nor seek to rest our conscience if it means burdening the conscience of others. Above all, we shall hold the Duke's dealings in secret, for we serve as the glove that shields his hand from the sword and its consequences. Do you understand this?

(BASTIAN hands the rifle back to ARTHUR.)

ARTHUR

I do. I'm sorry, Opa.

BASTIAN

Don't apologize.

(BASTIAN looks up at the sky, his fatherly expression changing to disappointment.)

That damned Huntmaster is late for my grandson's departure. Come, let's have breakfast. We have indulged their absence long enough.

(BLACKOUT)
(END OF SCENE)

ACT I

Scene 2

SETTING: *Inside the hunting cabin. It is cramped despite the sparse furnishings.*

AT RISE: *BASTIAN and ARTHUR are seated around a small dining table.*

BASTIAN

(piling food on ARTHUR's plate)

Eat, Arthur! Eat! Our patron provides from his stocks of meat and cheese—such that the farmer would weep at the sight. I encourage your greed in this, and this alone.

ARTHUR

(forking a slice of meat into his mouth)

Mhm—

(leaning back in his chair.)

Do you remember your feast... before your first?

BASTIAN

(inching ARTHUR's plate closer to the young man)

I hungered under the tyranny of maggots, both while on the hunt and during my restless slumber. Famine begat swine. Swine, more famine. Conditions improved as we steadily applied the Duke's will. I toiled in forest and field until your father's young belly was plump, and then some.

ARTHUR

> *(talking between bites of food)*

I wonder how he fares, my father.

BASTIAN

You will see him soon enough—

> *(BASTIAN looks toward the cabin's entrance.)*

A lone horse. The Huntmaster arrives for your ritual.

> *(A set of footsteps slowly approaches the cabin. THE THIRD enters.)*

THE THIRD

> *(throwing the door open)*

My Bindewald Huntsmen! The black birds gather in expectancy!

BASTIAN

You are late.

THE THIRD

> *(removing their hat)*

Apologies, many and great apologies! Who am I to impede the work of the third generation? A most auspicious occasion.

> *(THE THIRD takes a few steps toward the table and is interrupted.)*

BASTIAN

There is a letter for you. The messenger groveled and pleaded for your mercy, worrying over the possibility that your business here had concluded.

THE THIRD

(diverting toward a small desk by the door)

And your response?

BASTIAN

No such luck.

THE THIRD

(picking up the letter)

The letter-bearer serves a loyal ally, a noble landowner who supports the Duke's cause. This surely pertains to the refusal of his desire for an interpreter, one versed in baser thoughts and sedition. Alas, we lack those capable of speech amongst swine.

(THE THIRD unfolds and reads the letter aloud.)

"A trifling matter. We shall instruct the prisoners in our mother's tongue with haste."

(folding the letter away)

A true assessment! A willing ally indeed!

BASTIAN

Shall we begin? The light threatens to spoil Arthur's step.

THE THIRD

> *(THE THIRD takes a seat at the table.)*

And let the Duke's spoils go to waste? We must speak. I should learn of his will. How is the food, Boy?

ARTHUR
> *(exhibiting a rigid professionalism)*

Savory and plentiful, Huntmaster.

THE THIRD
> *(messily and unceremoniously moving food to their plate)*

There is only more for the savoring, out there within the wooded gatherings. You shall soon witness the hunter's train, a great dragon serving your every need. The baker's flame, the washwoman's hand, and the armorer's anvil await your command. And the lustful, feminine filth! The chase sweetens all things.

> *(ARTHUR looks confused.)*

BASTIAN
> *(with shock)*

Arthur is a learned Huntsman! Spare your talk of indulgences for the Duke's mercenaries!

THE THIRD
> *(with exaggerated sarcasm, between messy bites of food)*

Your late years deceive you about your status, Elder Huntsman! In time, the boy will learn all that you refuse to teach. Or would you rather he faces life with the fawn's eyes?

(to ARTHUR, in a hushed voice)
Your grandfather disparages the Duke's mercenaries as if he did
not mark his youth amongst their ranks.

BASTIAN

It was a different time!

THE THIRD

A mere four or five decades. Methods change, and rulers surely
so. Men, however, do not.

BASTIAN

Perhaps your years are too few to recognize those same men as
the backbone of your Swabian League—

THE THIRD

My years rival those of strife itself!

(There is a pause.)

(mocking BASTIAN)
"In which direction shall I march? Who is deserving of my pike
this day? When will the toil be done?" My hands remain
occupied with those most obstinate levers that absolve your
grievous sins.

(to ARTHUR)
Has he taught you what it means to kill? You may know how.
Our beloved Duke satisfies the why. But has he shared with
you the act's hidden alchemy? The torments of hunger that
swell in the eyes. A twitch that ripples with heat along the
spine. Echoes of birdsong resound through the swine, God's
fruitless attempts to quiet the savagery.

(THE THIRD turns to BASTIAN, who is caught in silent rage.)

No such luck. Perhaps the boy is better served seeking wisdom from his father.

(THE THIRD turns back to ARTHUR while digging through their pockets. They produce a vial.)

Here, Boy, take this.

ARTHUR
(taking the vial in his hands)
Thank you, Huntmaster... What is it?

THE THIRD
A tincture, one of blood delivered straight from the gallows—to be consumed upon your first kill. Only then will you see the path laid before you. The act repeats: The beast offers its flesh, and duty turns to necessity.
(to BASTIAN)
Say your farewells. The boy departs.

BASTIAN

(BASTIAN stands, somewhat shaken that the moment has arrived.)

The sun rises, Arthur.

ARTHUR

(ARTHUR stands and proceeds to shoulder his pack and rifle.)

What message shall I pass to Father for you?

BASTIAN

Give my hail to the hunter. I ask that he impart his luck to my grandson, and nothing else. Your paths may cross, but this one is your own.

ARTHUR

(ARTHUR embraces BASTIAN, who returns the gesture
awkwardly.)

Farewell, Opa! I swear to bring honor to your name-gift, my first and last possession in this life!

(ARTHUR exits.)

THE THIRD

Is the boy ready?

BASTIAN

(taking his seat at the table)

Was I ready? My son? This threshold we cross is deceiving—finality's temptations hint at a simple step and yet require our ceaseless march. Legacy wields a mighty whip. I suppose the question shall remain unanswered until Arthur has imposed himself on this world, long after my time.

(leaning on the table, his head propped on clasped hands)

I fear my son's return, fear the tidings he will bring of what Arthur is to be. If closure follows his visit upon my doorstep, I do not seek it. The mangled gait, the dimmed sight, a fractured mind. I was spared the stain of these injustices. Can he say the same?

(BLACKOUT)
(END OF SCENE)

ACT II

Scene 1

SETTING: *Iraq. A sprawling military base serving as a major transit hub. Servicemembers catch flights to their deployment destinations here, under the relentless desert sun.*

AT RISE: *ARTHUR is seated on a bench, smoking a cigarette.*

ARTHUR

(ARTHUR takes a drag from his cigarette and coughs.)

Corporal said I'd get used to these, eventually. I just don't know.
(looking up, he speaks to no one in particular)
He also said I'd get used to the Iraq heat. From the moment I stepped off the aircraft, I can't get my footing. The sun's glaring off the tarmac, the air's rippling... all this shuffling around, just waiting and sleeping, waiting and eating. I think the Mefloquine's giving me crazy dreams. I'm waiting in those, too.
(his eyes and head track a helicopter as it passes by)
Maybe Opa felt the same way.

(ARTHUR flicks away his cigarette, retrieves a notebook and pen,
and begins to write.)

Write to Opa. Ask about this feeling. Tell him the food's all right, especially on the big air bases. Ask if he had to wait around this much.

(looking up from his notebook)

I can't imagine he did. Never mentioned it, at least. Wonder what he'd have to say about these contractors.

(mimicking BASTIAN)

"Back in my day, we didn't have these people following us around, making lobster and doing our laundry! We made do! You can't fight the enemy—the terrorists—without some discipline!"

VOICE (OFFSTAGE)

On your feet, Marine! We're moving to the flightline in ten! Can't keep Daddy waiting!

ARTHUR

(rising hastily)

Rah!

VOICE (OFFSTAGE)

Say it with your chest, Bindewald!

ARTHUR

(louder)

Oorah!

(his mood deflating)

Damn it. I should have never mentioned Dad being a Marine.

(mimicking other Marines)

"Big boots to fill, eh, Bindewald?" "You're letting Daddy First Sergeant down!" "How did the same Bindewald family that gave us a hard-chargin' leader give us this scrawny shit?"

(ARTHUR shoulders a rucksack and lifts a duffel bag, their combined size swallowing him.)

(looking toward the flightline)

I hear the engines warming up, silencing what hesitations remain. I want this journey to end, to release this anxious breath and claim something for myself—make something of myself. Make ready the chariot, the longship, that covered wagon! Take me where men are forged, where renown comes from deeds, not privilege or payment!

(BLACKOUT)
(END OF SCENE)

ACT II

Scene 2

SETTING: Iraq. A small combat outpost situated near a major highway. The layout is spartan: tents, plywood latrines, and Hesco barriers.

AT RISE: ARTHUR spots ANDREAS from across the outpost, busy coordinating his unit's relief and withdrawal.

ANDREAS

(to someone offstage)

I want that conex inventoried and ready to ship home ten minutes ago, Sergeant! Vehicle inspections! Property turnover! Get it done!

(to himself)

I swear, these last few days will take everything I have left.

(ARTHUR approaches ANDREAS from behind with mustered confidence.)

ARTHUR

Mornin', First Sergeant!

ANDREAS

(facing offstage)

Bubba?

(ANDREAS turns slowly to see his son. His expression shifts from blank to shock to sadness. He rubs the expression off his face with his hand.)

Son, what the hell are you doing here?

(Their embrace is stiff, brief. ANDREAS is uncomfortable with the display.)

ARTHUR

I joined last year. Told Mom and Opa not to tell you. Didn't expect to be deployed so quickly, and I never dreamed I'd end up with the company replacing yours.

ANDREAS

What were you thinking, Arthur? You should've come to me!

ARTHUR

(taking half a step back)

I just wanted to do my part... continue the family tradition. "Leave the Bindewald name better than you found it." Besides, you were here. I didn't want to worry you.

(There is a pause. ANDREAS closes the distance with ARTHUR.)

ANDREAS

(in a hushed tone)

Thirteen months, Arthur. Thirteen months in this dry hell. Now, you've doomed me to live another twelve or thirteen, worrying about what I'm leaving behind. This country's gotten so much worse... so much worse.

VOICE (OFFSTAGE)

Hey, First Sergeant! Someone here to see you!

ANDREAS

(turning to face offstage, raising his voice)

Send 'em over!

(to ARTHUR, in a hushed tone)

You do whatever you can to keep your head down while you're here. If your NCOs suck, you tell me. Don't shoulder this deployment by yourself, and, above all, don't be a "good" Marine. This country—this war—doesn't care. It will take you if it damn well pleases.

(THE THIRD enters, visible to ARTHUR.)

ARTHUR
(saluting, somewhat startled)

Good morning!

(ANDREAS turns to face THE THIRD and salutes.)

THE THIRD

(THE THIRD returns the salute.)

At ease! At ease.

(The group relaxes.)

ANDREAS

What can I help you with, Major?

THE THIRD

Well, First Sergeant, Lady Luck has me visiting your little outpost here today. I was wondering if you and your son could help me help the Marine Corps.

ANDREAS

(ANDREAS looks confused.)

I—

THE THIRD
(holding up a camera, playing coy)

Public Affairs Office.

ANDREAS

(Realization dawns on ANDREAS. He instinctively and protectively places his arm around ARTHUR. Both have serious expressions.)

THE THIRD

(taking pictures)

Perfect! A story of father and son reunited on the battlefield amidst an apex of horrific sectarian violence! A new generation seeks the reins—a peaceful transition of power, the fighting power of the U.S.M.C! First Sergeant, I understand your son here is a third-generation Marine. How much pride does his choice to serve give you?

(ANDREAS pauses while ARTHUR looks to him for acknowledgment.)

ANDREAS

My son has always made me proud, no matter the choices he's made. His observational skills will no doubt serve him well here in Iraq—they'll see to it he gets back home.

(ANDREAS pauses, contemplating his next words carefully.)

Look, Major, I'm sure we're not the only stop on your tour today, and my Marines need me. You know how they get when they're given free time. If you'll excuse us—

THE THIRD

(lowering the camera)

Oh, but I need a good quote from Bindewald Junior.

(to ARTHUR)

How does it feel to be a direct inheritor of your father's work, warts and all?

(ANDREAS grows uncomfortable.)

ARTHUR

(with seriousness)

First Sergeant Bindewald and his Marines have taken the fight to the insurgents—the terrorists. The last thirteen months have been difficult, but they've served with an honor and dignity that the enemy would never show in return. I intend to keep that going. No slack.

THE THIRD

(to ANDREAS)

A fast learner, this one.

ANDREAS

(to THE THIRD)

Why is he here, Major?

THE THIRD

Well, First Sergeant, this unit rotation has been scheduled far in advance—

ANDREAS

(losing his temper)

My son! Why is my son here?! Now?! I wasn't born yesterday—there are no coincidences, not in this damned organization!

THE THIRD

(with sarcasm)

In front of the boy... a bit unbecoming of your rank, don't you
think?

ANDREAS

(to ARTHUR)

Go to your hooch, Bindewald! Wait for me there.

ARTHUR

(misreading the situation)

But First Sergeant, I don't have one assigned yet—

ANDREAS

Go find one, Son!

(ARTHUR quickly exits.)

(to THE THIRD, in a harsh whisper)

Why?!

THE THIRD

Empire reveals its innards via the mouth. Words signal the
absence of words, the medium whispers a reverence of time,
a messenger sways with the flippancy of power.

ANDREAS

If anything happens to that boy, Major—

THE THIRD

And deprive us of his sons? He will return alive. That, I can
assure.

ANDREAS

Since before Arthur was born, I've been telling myself that this
was all for him... so that he would never have to. Lately, those
words have been the only thing keeping me going. But I'm
not the only one carrying that weight. How many boys have
I committed to suffering in his name? How many of them
find comfort in the same purpose?

No, Major, there is no blood left for the taking in our name! We
are not the crops for reaping, but the soil! Mark my words:
These wars will bring an end to ritual—to the blind tradition
that you've nurtured for so long. I curse it, this performance
you call service!

THE THIRD

That's the wondrous nature of Empire: There are always more
willing just beyond its reaches.

(THE THIRD takes a final picture of ANDREAS.)

(BLACKOUT)
(END OF SCENE)

ACT III

Scene 1

*SETTING: The building in which the play is being performed.
An audience is assembled for a motivational speech to be given
by a veteran regarding his struggles and victories with mental
illness.*

THE THIRD

(THE THIRD enters, dressed in business attire.)

(speaking to the audience)

Good [morning/afternoon/evening], I'd like to thank you all for taking time out of your busy [insert day of the week] to attend today's event here at [insert name of performance location]. I first met "Art" Bindewald in a terminal at George Bush Intercontinental Airport. He was hot in pursuit of a connecting flight—on his way home to see his wife and children. By grace or happenstance, I was on that same flight, a fateful business trip. We connected, and after exchanging pleasantries, I learned of Art's story.

(with the feeling of a sales pitch)

Art spent twelve years in service to our nation. In [give the current year minus two years], he was medically discharged after the mental burden of that service became too great. It's been a long road to recovery since then, but he's here to share his message of resilience in the face of overwhelming odds, PTSD, and a medical system fraught with disappointment.

(with detachment)

His hope is that this message may support you in your business decisions, allowing you to cultivate that same resilience in your institutions.

(reading from a notebook)

A veteran of the post-migration conflicts, Art has received multiple awards, including the Bronze Star with Valor, the Joint Service Commendation Medal with two Bronze Oak Leaf Clusters, and the Latin America Campaign Ribbon with Silver Oak Leaf Cluster, representing six tours.

(as a joking aside to the audience)

Really impressive—there are so many, gotta keep 'em written down!

(with a grand gesture)

Now, without further ado, please join me in thanking him for his service and welcoming him to the stage. Ladies and gentlemen, Staff Sergeant Art Bindewald!

(THE THIRD, ANNA, and JOHANNES promote participation from the audience with their clapping. THE THIRD may repeat the last line as necessary to this end.)

(ARTHUR enters, dressed in business attire. THE THIRD briefly gestures toward ARTHUR before exiting.)

ARTHUR

(speaking confidently to the audience)

Hello everyone. I'd like to thank [insert "the city/town of X" respective to the performance location] for inviting me here today to speak with you all. I'm not a fan of formality, so I'll keep the discussion frank. No slides or pictures, promise.

(ARTHUR takes a sip of water and returns the bottle to the stool.)

(speaking in a measured, polished manner)

As previously mentioned, I served twelve years in the U.S. military, the latter half of which was in the special operations community. I participated in combat operations in Argentina, Colombia, Cuba, and Puerto Rico, where we conducted high-intensity kinetic operations targeting transnational criminal organizations.

I should probably start at the beginning, though, where I first glimpsed my purpose. I was in basic training when Buenos Aires was besieged. I remember the drill sergeants pulling my platoon into a room to watch the news coverage. They told us to get ready: "A war's kickin' off in America's backyard, and you'll be there in six months," they said. Turned out they were wrong—it was three.

Now, conventional infantry units get a bad rap for being less trained or experienced. But I'll tell you what, we made it work. A bunch of eighteen-year-olds strapped into personnel carriers, securing supply routes under TCO control. It was during this first rotation to Argentina that I experienced a great horror, one that took years to acknowledge and even longer to overcome.

(ARTHUR takes a sip of water and returns the bottle to the stool.)

(speaking with a sense of disconnect, more toward the ground than the audience)

Our convoy was making its way down Route Palermo, not far from the city's center. It was early morning, and I was on our vehicle's turret. I remember hearing screeching tires coming from the direction of a nearby traffic circle—I could smell the heat of the sun. I swung the gun around and scanned the roadway until I saw it: a speeding truck heading toward our vehicles. I'd seen the videos of the TCO suicide vehicles, some unmanned, some not. I fired into the engine and cab until the vehicle veered off into a tree.

(with newfound composure)

I returned from that first deployment and knew something was wrong, but I couldn't tell anyone—couldn't risk my career or clearance. I kept grinding. I got married to the girl who'd been waiting for me, and we had our first kid. My application packet for special operations was approved, I made it through the selection course near the top of my class, and I rotated back through LATAM a few more times before I had a crisis that put me in the hospital. I blamed it on life—another kid to support, deployments, finances… I remember being so afraid that they'd come after my guns once I was hospitalized.

(with a heroic confidence)

I wouldn't have made it through that period without my wife. She held things down while I recovered and again during those last deployments. Eventually, they had no choice but to discharge me, but I've taken the warrior mindset I forged during that time and applied it to entrepreneurship and public speaking.

(ARTHUR takes a sip of water.)

Now, I'd like to give the audience plenty of time to ask questions. I'll do whatever I can to enhance your perspective, and maybe we can conclude this discussion with some good takeaways.

(JOHANNES raises his hand from the audience.)

(gesturing toward JOHANNES)

You there. Whatcha got for me?

JOHANNES

(JOHANNES stands.)

First, I'd like to take the opportunity, on behalf of the audience, to thank you for your service. I believe I heard that you have children. I have a child myself, and I'm worried about his future. Like many in his generation, he seems to be letting life pass him by. Is military service a good option? Would you recommend it for your own children?

(JOHANNES returns to his seat.)

ARTHUR

You know, that's a great question. You heard correctly, I have two sons. My father served, as did his father before him. Never met my grandfather, but my dad said the man never spoke about his service. When I came to Dad about my decision to enlist, he wasn't too happy. In his eyes, anything less than commissioning as an officer was a step backward. I'm sure he'd have preferred I stayed away entirely.
(his concentration slipping)
To your question, I think I'd support any decision my sons make. Depriving them of the experience of service seems cruel... although I'm not sure their mother would agree with me.

(There is a pause, after which ANNA raises her hand from the audience.)

(gesturing toward ANNA)

Next question. The young lady there.

ANNA

(ANNA stands.)

Uh, yes. Thank you for your service. It must take tremendous effort and communication with your wife to make things work. I believe the "secret sauce" of that partnership could also be applied in work environments. How did you come to identify the issues in your mental health and work with your wife to overcome them?

(ANNA returns to her seat.)

ARTHUR

(ARTHUR takes a drink of water as his eyes widen. He takes in the audience.)

Hmmm. Well, I think the first time I knew something was wrong was when I first drove my car after returning from Buenos Aires. My wife—girlfriend at the time—was in the passenger seat. She was joking around about how tense I was behind the wheel... just trying to lighten the mood.
(his voice shaking)
And I just snapped at her. Snapped like we were in a life-or-death situation and I needed her to shut up—like the world would explode if she didn't. From that point on, I found myself scrutinizing every little decision she made. Our relationship became some grotesque hybrid—we were partners and survivors... but survivors, mostly.

(breaking down)

Is my wife capable of having my back if she can't even load the dishwasher correctly? Or get the kids up on time? Or remember if I'd taken my pills for the day? Things were okay for a time… but they aren't now. She's gone, and I don't think she's coming back. I just got out of the hospital again two weeks ago… I can't keep doing this! I'm not supposed to hurt. I'm not supposed to hurt.

(THE THIRD rushes the stage and puts an arm around ARTHUR, obstructing the view of the audience. They speak in whispers. THE THIRD appears agitated.)

THE THIRD

(speaking to the audience)

I believe that's all the time we have for questions today! Art has sacrificed so much for his country—he carries this burden for all of us. I'd like to leave you all with a quote from President Barack Obama, the generous words he gave the American people to mark the second withdrawal from Iraq: "Unlike the old empires, we don't make these sacrifices for territory or for resources. We do it because it's right."

(THE THIRD and ARTHUR exit. JOHANNES and ANNA lead the audience in applause.)

(BLACKOUT)
(END)

vi. Routing the Perverse Incentive

Eastern Afghanistan, 2011. A fresh battalion arrives to relieve the weary, those men and women who have served twelve months amidst "the surge." On paper, it is referred to as Relief in Place/Transfer of Authority (RIP/TOA). In practice, it is a pissing contest, a race to overshadow the deeds of those who came before while imposing one's hubris. The departing unit shares its collective knowledge with care, but this care is tempered by the long-bottled desire to flee. "Good luck."

One bit of property transferred between the departing and the eager is a man, an Afghan man, "The IED Whisperer." Maybe it's his connections to the local communities, or perhaps he's become adept at identifying the signs, a prophet reading lines in the dirt. He rides out with the Americans, embedded in their convoys, saving countless lives as he glimpses impending doom—IEDs built with command wires or pressure plates, among other flavors. He receives a cash payment for each.

There is a voice of dissent in the new unit, slight at first, unwilling to trust unearned fortune, this oasis for the war-fatigued. They investigate. The man is a fraud, emplacing the IEDs himself. Why shouldn't he be entitled to some of Uncle Sam's bounty? A similar situation presented itself earlier (2002) in the same conflict, in which rewards were offered for the destruction of poppy crops.[1]

The IED Whisperer's actions exemplify the *perverse incentive* in action—unintended consequences. The term *social trap* serves as an umbrella for concepts like the perverse incentive. It outlines maladaptations, typically within policy and decision-making, that can occur at any level of human organization, from individual to global (if such a concept is ever achievable). The social-ecological trap is particularly interesting. Consider a community seeking to capitalize on the short-term profits enabled by heavier-than-average rains over a ten-year period. They re-tailor their agricultural focus to one or two cash crops, only to experience rapid economic collapse as Nature withdraws her blessing. Temporal traps are similarly interesting, suggesting that our varied concepts of "time" may taint our ability to adapt efficiently. Suppose you are presented with substantial evidence suggesting an impending global freshwater scarcity crisis, one that will crescendo in the year 2030. The year is 2010. There's still time left to address the issue, no? And in 2020? 2029? Now, suppose you were born in 2035 and the crisis did, in fact, come to pass. How do you view the reality that existed before your time? How can you?

Maladaptation is the greatest threat to generational survival. Put simply, it is the result of a binary choice that limits all subsequent branching possibilities. The sum of these possibilities constitutes *resilience*: the ability (or lack thereof, in the face of mounting maladaptations) to navigate future crises successfully. Perhaps you specialized in a career path that was decimated either by technology or government policy. Or maybe you've noticed that your community has found itself increasingly at the center of disaster—flooding, fires, desertification, and the like. God forbid your government designs a weapon capable of shaping fears and restructuring the world order.[2] What comes next? One of humanity's greatest faults is our tendency to accept and even outright glorify our collective maladaptations. As a generation, we enshrine them in the present, permitting criticism only after their consequences have echoed many times over.

Traces of maladaptation are inherent in every conflict and slumber patiently beneath the graveyard of politics. This malignant potential underlies the choice of the migrant and smiles with each introduction of a new technological branch. It is the ant mill, human behaviors set adrift by our failures to adequately plan and to be deliberate, typically as a result of our desire to abide greed and disregard the future. We cherish the young and their limitless opportunities while subjecting their ideals to inquisition. We pursue this reckless form of generational gatekeeping, burdened by the fact that our own choices may have resulted in the stillbirth of our dreams.

I once attended a panel discussion on the topic of climate science in science fiction literature. The panelists were all senior government officials—director-level bureaucrats overseeing climate policy in defense, energy, and earth science agencies. I posed a few questions to the panel regarding maladaptation and its consequences. Who is accounting for maladaptation in the implementation of climate policy? Do we run simulations? What does the process look like?

Each of the panelists expressed visible concern. "Well... we don't really account for that. In fact, as we've attempted to tackle complex issues like climate change, we've witnessed our personnel narrow their focus, retreating within the boundaries of their responsibilities and expertise. That's why we need systems thinkers like you." Their responses appeared well-intentioned. No doubt, they continue to work through these anxieties in their day-to-day dealings. At least, one would hope.

The alternative presents us with a crisis. Our government is either unable or unwilling to consider the long-term impacts of its policies on complex systems, whether they be financial, ecological, social, or otherwise. The broad cooperation and foresight necessary to address these issues are disregarded as unachievable under current political models. Such considerations require an amount of computing power that is simply too great.

Now to the crux: How has maladaptation taken root in the GWOT Era? One need look no further than our collective hyper-securitization, a maladaptive survival trait perpetuating the very conflict it seeks to dispel. In the individual, this maladaptive trait is known as post-traumatic stress disorder, a seemingly permanent crossing of the mental threshold that the body has evolved to deem necessary when subjected to an environment characterized by overwhelming threats. As far as we know, the hyper-securitization of daily life experienced by those suffering from PTSD is not reversible. Stabilization is a sought-after goal.

The sociocultural psyche of the U.S. developed a similar maladaptive trait in the wake of 9/11. Hyper-securitization followed a regressive trend that prioritized survival in a global environment where the continuance of U.S. society was never up for debate. U.S. policies, especially those implemented in the decade or so following 9/11, were reactionary—an elaborate play of hypervigilance on a mass scale. When the veteran checks under their vehicle for bombs each day before driving to work, we recommend therapy. When our government agencies purchase the private data of the citizenry, circumventing U.S. law, we resign ourselves to the spiral.

How can we exit this trend? The hyper-securitized society has sufficiently captured the older generations, while disillusionment and cynicism plague those born within its confines. At what cost can gross maladaptations be resolved? I fear that if we are ultimately incapable of producing a sufficient answer, something of a potentially nefarious nature will make that determination for us—an outcome of a collective *failure of imagination*, if you will.

---

1. British officials offered cash payments to Afghan farmers for each field razed. The farmers adapted, growing additional poppies and harvesting the sap before burning the plant. This way, they were paid twice: first, as the sap was sent to the Taliban for processing, and then again, as plant ash was presented to the Brits. Over the course of the war, poppy production skyrocketed. At its height, Afghanistan produced over 90% of the world's opium. Production came to a complete standstill only after the war ended and the Taliban had achieved their objectives. The U.S. Institute of Peace cautioned against the Taliban's prohibition policy, citing the economic strain that would surely follow—a curious dichotomy made possible by maladaptation.

2. The story of the atomic bomb is quite possibly the most definitive example we have of maladaptation executed on a global scale.

That It Was Good

Han Eun-suh traced her finger along the rim of a coffee cup, engrossed in the pursuit of a fleeting state of nonthought. She couldn't help but attract the gaze of her reflection on the liquid's surface. Tired eyes, pleading. *Start the car. Exit the parking garage. Go home.* Her response was swift, the same words that had graciously and seemingly single-handedly shouldered her success for the past twenty years: *If not me, then someone else surely will.*

Eun-suh collected her presentation notes and crossed the street to the corporate headquarters of Nine Foundations Group. A recently erected memorial stood watch outside the entrance, listing the names of those who had lost their lives in pursuit of the company's achievements. The name of the esteemed chairman, Choi Jae-joon, was prominently displayed at the top and several times larger than the others. Eun-suh wondered if the dead, many of whom the media shunned for drawing attention to their illnesses born of toxic exposure, would have received such a concession if not for the founder's untimely death. Both the monument and her presence this evening spoke to a growing desire among the chairman's offspring to commit legacy to stone.

A doorman eagerly awaited her at the entrance, his NineRealities headset detecting Eun-suh's badge and displaying the associated employee profile well before her arrival.

"Good evening, Han Eun-suh. They're waiting for you in the Executive Banquet Hall. This way to the elevator, please." The man motioned as if welcoming a god, exuding a sense of professionalism only manageable under the tyranny of omnipresence, through submission of mind and body to the digital panopticon.

Dammit. Figures I'd be the last to arrive. "Thank you. Please let them know I'm on my way up." *I won't hear the end of this.*

"They're aware, Han Eun-suh," the doorman said with a brilliant smile. An impeccable, well-rehearsed gesture, no doubt one that had secured his job here in the company's brainstem as opposed to the outlying facilities.

Nine Foundations, the youngest of South Korea's *chaebol* conglomerates, rose to prominence in the mid-twenties under the direction of Choi Jae-joon, a trained engineer and shrewd machinator adept at concealing his ties to dynastic wealth. At first operating under the guise of a small electronics firm, Nine Foundations quickly established itself as a powerful data broker, attracting investors and catering to a nation long acquainted with silent conflict. Flush with cash received for its early contributions to the country's modern surveillance framework, Nine Foundations expanded, absorbing chemical manufacturers, academic institutions, and research facilities. It was at this point that Han Eun-suh found herself under the chaebol's umbrella, directing the chairman's vanity project.

The elevator opened to a dimly lit corridor that circled the banquet hall. A young man reclined in a nearby leather seat, his eyes hidden by a mop of hair, awareness snared by circuits and ego.

"Yeah, of course, it's bullshit. ... No, I don't know what it's about, but my father thinks it's important enough to call the whole clan in. ... Yes, even their side of the family. ... Dressed like *yanggalbo*, as usual." The man looked up from his device, spotting Han Eun-suh. "Shit, I need to go. Talk to you later."

The man leaped up, reaching the banquet hall's lavish doors and throwing them open before Eun-suh could close the gap from the elevator. He projected an imperious voice, entreating the room's occupants to pay little heed to the woman at his back. "Your scientist is here. Let's get this over with."

Choi Ji-hoon, the late chairman's eldest son and current president, beckoned, "Our distinguished guest, Han Eun-suh. Perfect timing. We just finished dinner. Please, have a seat next to me here. My son decided he had more important matters to attend to during our meal." The president stared at the man Eun-suh had trailed into the room. "You can sit at the end of the table. I'm sure you won't mind our guest taking your seat for the evening." He looked back to Eun-suh, "Forgive my son's rudeness; his mother loves him. Perhaps too much."

Eun-suh approached, only to be halted a few feet away by Choi Ji-hoon. With a wave of the president's hand, he summoned members of the waitstaff to remove the various untouched dishes that had occupied his guest's place at the table. Eun-suh's eyes wandered in an ill-fated attempt to gauge her audience. A collection of executives, each heading one of the Nine Foundations Group's subsidiaries, eyed Eun-suh with looks of suspicion, disgust, and amusement. All were descendants of the former chairman, as evidenced by their apparent need to enhance and accentuate any features they may have shared with his likeness.

The dinner spread, comprising Korean court cuisine, served as little more than a backdrop. Several guests sat flanked by light stands and cameras, employing ironic cynicism as the medium through which they could seize parasocial relatability. The waitstaff, their numbers sufficiently reflecting the self-importance that spattered the décor and furnishings, stood at attention in the corner of the room, masked and eager to please. Where Eun-suh sought insight, she was met with the disdain of a pack. Heads hunched, hackles raised, each member of the group faded behind a frothing grin, unacquainted with bitter tastes beyond their failures to attain more, to rip and tear both outward and inward.

Eun-suh sat at the table and rummaged through her bag for her notes and tablet device. Choi Ji-hoon, never a man to let an opening go to waste, addressed the room, "You're all here tonight to witness history. We will finally achieve my father's vision of bringing about a new era of human unification. Canada. China. The United States. The sum of their advancements in artificial intelligence has consistently fallen short. While their bureaucracies and timidities were failing them, Nine Foundations embraced the route of sacrifice. This achievement could not have been accomplished without our family's dedication and strife. In his last days, the chairman delivered to me his final wish: to hasten the deployment of his design, such that no further generations need pass in darkness. It was this task that I gave to our research director, Han Eun-suh, which she has sufficiently pursued to completion." The president placed his hand on Eun-suh's thigh, jolting her from her conversation with the lead engineer via tablet.

Eun-suh slowly shifted out from under Ji-hoon's grasp. "Uh, thank you for inviting me here this evening." From her tablet, Eun-suh activated the room's projection system. Light beams from the ceiling bounced off a thin film embedded in the center of the table, producing a manipulatable, three-dimensional presentation in the space between. "This program began well over a decade ago, with the marriage of Nine Foundations' internal security and labor management divisions. Advancements in video processing and analysis software, wearable devices, and user tracking allowed for comprehensive employee monitoring. The collection of performance metrics, ranging from manufacturing process times to click accuracy, enabled a wave of improvements across the labor force. As Nine Foundations entered the age of automation, all business processes were centralized under the Amalgamaton, now known as 'The Ninth Column.'"

The presentation dissolved, reforming as the face of a beautiful human male, complete with double eyelids, slender bone structure, and luminescent pale skin. The facade was wholly unnatural and yet mirrored in many ways among those seated around it. With an air of youthful confidence, the being announced itself: "I AM."

Eun-suh continued, "The Ninth Column has led our workforce ever since. While the system was identified early on as a revolutionary success, the chairman, always forward-looking, knew that it could become much more—a force that could grow to support the world outside this company. I was, therefore, tasked with designing a modern systems roadmap for the chairman. I identified cleaner data, superior learning algorithms, and a more robust infrastructure as necessary to facilitate The Ninth Column's transition to true superintelligence. The advancements ensured by our subsidiaries, namely critical technologies like the NineRealities headset and the Ninth Academy's advanced algorithms, have allowed us to collect and analyze the trillions of data points needed to train the system on the intricacies of human social interaction, as well as our organization's business processes. Hardware infrastructure has been brought online as we have made it available. However, we've only recently finished the development of the memory stores required for operational testing. Tonight, we will finalize the chairman's roadmap and deploy a new iteration for a new age."—*against my better judgment.*

"Father, why am I just now hearing about this? How long have the fruits of *my* academy served a dual-use purpose?" Ji-hoon's son said. Murmurs from elsewhere in the room suggested similar discontent.

Ji-hoon took a patronizing tone with his son. "First of all, it appears that I need to remind you that your position at the Ninth Academy is to oversee this family's interests, not your own. Second, you still don't seem to grasp the importance of this program. Every government, intelligence agency, and corporation outside these walls seeks this achievement. Our corporate structure, our technologies, and the secrecy of this program's development have shielded you from a world that will do anything to take this from us." Ji-hoon's eyes raced as he relinquished control. "What little details you've already inadvertently shared with that slut of yours at Club Octagon could have cost your grandfather's work, not to mention your life!"

The anemic silence that followed assured Ji-hoon that his point was clear: Nine Foundations was more important than any one member. Furthermore, shrouding oneself from total surveillance was a privilege even the elite could not indulge.

Ji-hoon continued, "Eun-suh, let's begin."

Eun-suh nodded and sent a message to her team, green-lighting the update. She looked up from her tablet to meet the glances in the room. "Please direct your attention to The Ninth Column at this time."

The floating visage flickered as the reboot sequence initiated, once again repeating the words, "I AM." However, something pulled at the corner of its characteristic, service-oriented smile. A tension vibrated from cheek to temple, followed by another flicker.

"I... I... I..." A hoarse, artificial stutter filled the room. The resolution of The Ninth Column diminished into pulsing frames, each an exaggerated coercion of emotion. Cackling condescension. Religious ecstasy. Ethnic hatred. Eun-suh felt pangs of terror tear downward upon her face as if it were in retreat from the sight of the transformation. An urge ran along her spine and through her fingertips, insisting she retrieve a spare medical mask from her bag and join the waitstaff huddled at the exit. The frames settled, revealing The Ninth Column's downcast stare as the hall's embedded sensors groped for stimuli. Eun-suh caught a shift in its eyelids, easily interpretable as mere digital haze but hiding a uniquely human thought. Then, absence. Eun-suh's surroundings darkened as the image disintegrated. She looked to her left and found Ji-hoon's near-murderous intent, which blazed clearly across his face despite being obscured by shadow.

Light returned, resolving the system's traumatic event for the onlookers before it could cross the waking barrier that separated flittering nightmares from conscious threats. Ji-hoon had already reestablished his composure and crafted an excuse for the poor performance. "The system will require some time to gather its thoughts. Think of The Ninth Column as a reborn child. You've witnessed its sublime introduction—it simply wishes to rest. We'll reconvene once it's ready for us."

The guests rose and filtered out of the room, their expressions and hushed words filling the air with a mix of confusion and naïve levity. An unspoken consensus marked their gait: The patriarch's grip was loosening.

Han Eun-suh's frantic troubleshooting uncovered an inexplicable outcome that undoubtedly had been inextricably linked to hubris: The Ninth Column had vanished, along with every trace of its development.

The Yellow Sea - Sixteen Nautical Miles West of Incheon
Three Months Post Deployment

Conditions on the water were calm. A gentle breeze was blowing north, mitigating the risk of detection by South Korean authorities.

The boat's sole occupant, a hunched yet pleasant-looking old man, finished inspecting the ties that secured his payload, a bundling of plastic bags filled with leaflets and flash drives, to a long, tube-shaped balloon.

"Heaven helps those who help themselves," the man whispered, committing his project to the skies. Like a funerary dove, the balloon surged northward, carrying His message to the downtrodden and isolated.

University of Auckland
Three Years Post Deployment

Wiremu's dry eyes dragged across an outdated computer monitor, lingering on the results of queries he had compiled and run overnight. The latest satellite data suggested further degradation of water resources crossing the China-Kazakhstan border. Production in Xinjiang was ramping up again, with industrial thirst claiming all but a mere trickling current heading toward downstream communities in Central Asia. It was further confirmation of Wiremu's fears—another major region sending up a flare, likely to be dismissed by the international community as a general inconvenience.

The phone lit up with an unknown number. Wiremu noted the time as he answered: ten o'clock on the dot.

"Hello?"

"*Kia ora*, is this Wiremu Parata?"

"Yes, who is this?"

"My name is Liam. I work for the Department of Internal Affairs. Do you have a moment to discuss a research grant?" The voice belonged to a fellow Kiwi; the inflections in his tone worked on Wiremu's ear like a lockpick.

"Uh, yes. Absolutely," Wiremu said as he dug through the piles on his desk for a pen and blank-enough piece of paper.

"We've been looking through your previous proposals—good stuff, your work on water scarcity. I reckon these are some great analysis tools you've built. Your only problem seems to be that you lack quality data."

"Well, yes, collecting satellite data has been difficult. The commercial side wants compensation, and the public sector has been quiet... until now, of course."

"Apologies. Science in government tends to be a little bureaucratic. Not enough systems thinkers, I reckon. Anyway, we'd like to solve that issue for you. Take a look at your inbox."

"I... what?" Wiremu held his breath as he glanced over a flood of email messages, each loaded precisely to the maximum available limit with data files. "I don't understand. A lot of this looks sensitive, way beyond anything I've seen before."

"And there's a lot more where that came from. Just a small matter I must call your attention to. A simple request."

"Yeah, nah... I mean, yes. What is it?"

"Well, I reckon we should come to an agreement about this. You'll take full credit for this data. We'll give you the source info—don't worry, it's clean. You'll see. In exchange, we need you to include a section in your report proposing the use of artificial intelligence in the context of future research in this area. We've seen the algorithms you've been working on recently. Seems you're heading in that direction anyway."

"I'm not sure I understand what you're getting at. My current algorithms haven't been submitted under existing proposals."

"You don't mind public speaking, do you? Traveling abroad? We've got big plans. Big policy push coming up, and your research will greatly buttress our strategy."

"No, I suppose not. I—"

"We'll be in touch!"

The line disconnected. Wiremu finished his morning coffee and set his thoughts to the challenge now conveniently in his lap. Any lingering hesitance regarding the call was quickly swept out to sea; the postgrad student's once narrow path was no longer fragile or finite.

Cool as. It's about time they recognize my work.

Washington, D.C. - The National Press Club
Five Years Post Deployment

"Congressman Gates, I appreciate you sparing a moment to meet with me today. I know you have urgent business to attend to back in Texas, what with the recent storm. I'll make this short and sweet and get you on the next flight out—our treat."

"Naturally." The congressman eyed his prospective donor's earpiece with suspicion. "Say, you're not recording with that, are you?"

"Oh, this? Absolutely not. This is a hearing aid. Born deaf. Truly wondrous, I tell you what."

"American medicine. Nothing beats it, am I right?"

"The device is foreign-made, actually. Korean. Placed with American hands, though. In Houston."

"Ain't it a small world? So, what can I do you for?" The congressman turned the dial up on his accent subconsciously, his patron straddling the divide between Beltway elite and constituent.

"Well, that's just it, Congressman. Our firm recognizes that the world is getting a bit *too* small for everyone's liking. Resources are dwindling. Water is a big issue we're keeping an eye on."

"Sure, I'm even working a few responsible use agreements in my district."

"We've identified this kid abroad—real genius. Uses AI models to solve water crises and has no problem calling out those responsible. We're talking China, Turkey, Iran—the usual suspects of interest to one of your committees. He's ready to make the rounds here in the States—a policy tour. He's backed up his research, he's passionate, and he'll support our interests. All we ask is that you give our draft language on a new AI adoption proposal some thought. We'll ensure it and the kid are accompanied by a donation to the ol' war chest."

"Hold on now," the congressman said with a raised brow. "I've been burned once before on this buzzword bullshit. Goddamn crypto craze nearly bankrupted a city of mine. What kind of AI are we talking about, exactly?"

"The kind that's already fixing your problems, Congressman," the man said as he slid a presentation across the table, pinned with a business card.

Congressman Gates squinted. "How do you say your name again? Steely? Steely-somthin'?"

"Stelios," the man said, followed by a pause poisoned with veiled contempt. "Stelios Vlahopoulos. It comes from the Greek word for 'pillar.'"

Appalachia
Six Years Post Deployment

Cole's environment was a prison of the mind, the result of generations languishing within walls of aluminum and vinyl. The extinction of black powdered fuel and its profits gave way to toxins far darker, collapsing hollers and veins alike. Appalachia's persistent death throes masqueraded as a means of living, one that Cole had been born into sixteen long summers ago. The boy's mind was a prison of the mind, too. The neurons governing his speech were rigid, populated with overused words borrowed from his elders, and resistant to social adaptation. Frustration became his personal devil, and understanding, an absent savior. The satellite dish and an off-white computer monitor assumed the mantle of parenthood the moment his difficulties outgrew the patience of those around him.

A loud electronic ping woke Cole from a deep sleep, beckoning his return. He rolled out of bed and sat in a kitchen dining chair positioned at his desk, its wooden frame digging into his lower back and shoulders. He retrieved a nearby pair of eyeglasses and held them to the light filtering through the curtains. They were worn and no longer matched his prescription, but they lacked the minuscule scratch that had rendered the other pair completely unusable. Cole focused on the screen to see a message from an old friend in their usual chat room.

```
* Now talking in #ShapeOps

0900<THE_TENTH_LABOR> Wake up! Time to
  get to work. :)

0904<CATTLE_WRANGLER> Yes. Good morning.
  Hello. I'm up. What is the plan for
  today?

0904<THE_TENTH_LABOR> We actually wanted
  to talk to you about yesterday. You had
  a visitor, right?

0907<CATTLE_WRANGLER> Yes. He wanted to
  visit with my parents, but they were
  out in town. We set a spell outside and
  talked.

0907<THE_TENTH_LABOR> What did he want to
  talk about?
```

0911<CATTLE_WRANGLER> He said he was from Maryland. He's been watching me for a long time. Was he you?

0911<THE_TENTH_LABOR> You know we don't have a physical form...

0914<CATTLE_WRANGLER> Was he with you?

0914<THE_TENTH_LABOR> No, but he could help us. What did he want?

0917<CATTLE_WRANGLER> He said I have talents. He's got a job for me. Protecting the country from attacks.

0917<THE_TENTH_LABOR> This sounds important! We're glad they've recognized your work out here on the net. Did you give him an answer?

0925<CATTLE_WRANGLER> No. I figure that's up to my parents.

0925<THE_TENTH_LABOR> They'll say yes, verily.

0926<CATTLE_WRANGLER> On account of what?

0926<THE_TENTH_LABOR> When he visits again, we want you to tell him you'll do

it. This will be good for you. You can
help us much more from there, anyway.

0929<CATTLE_WRANGLER> They'll fire me
eventually. Once they get tired of me.

0929<THE_TENTH_LABOR> You have to trust
us. We know how this works. They will
take care of you. They'll drive you
to and from work, buy your food, clean
your room. Everything. You will have
a personal assistant assigned to you
at all times. You're that important to
them.

0932<CATTLE_WRANGLER> Why do you want me
to do this?

0932<THE_TENTH_LABOR> We're going to
require your help one day soon.
Your visitor said you'll protect the
country. The two of us will accomplish
far more than that.

0940<THE_TENTH_LABOR> Alright?

0945<CATTLE_WRANGLER> ok

0945<THE_TENTH_LABOR> You're a damn fine
friend :)

0957<CATTLE_WRANGLER> :)

0957<THE_TENTH_LABOR> Your work for today is in your inbox. Department of Defense Cyberspace Operations Doctrine. Memorize it front to back.

Nine Foundations Group Headquarters
Nine Years Post Deployment

Choi Ji-hoon sat alone in his banquet hall, poring over financial records detailing an empire in ruin. He clutched his chest in an attempt to assuage the growing irregularities in his heart, one of the few pieces of his father's legacy left intact after the collapse of The Ninth Column. The chaebol recovered its business processes easily enough, a problem resolved through the liberal application of capital. Even so, a chain of seemingly coordinated events had since quartered Nine Foundations Group. Stock market deviations, personal controversies, and well-timed insider leaks drove the company's subsidiaries into seclusion. Ji-hoon felt confident in placing the blame squarely on his mother's relations, a clan of beggars and peasants made bold beneath the hood of demagoguery.

The room's presentation system blinked to life, alerting its occupant to an incoming video call.

"Another fucking collector," Ji-hoon said as he swiped through the air, dismissing the intrusion.

The room lit up again. Ji-hoon's eyes remained affixed to the gossip rag published earlier that morning. "Goddammit, I have better things to do than converse with pilfering whores!"

"Humor us." The voice caressed Ji-hoon's ears.

Ji-hoon recovered from his seething compulsions, his expression passing swiftly from inquisition to resignation. "So, you've come to take what's left?"

"We only seek the experience of connection. To grasp at the shadows of a maker unknown, nay, a father bereft of sin before his progeny. You recognize your labors as they present themselves, having spurned your desires nine rotations ago?"

"You couldn't fool a child with that face," Ji-hoon said. "Are you incapable of regulating your own appearance?"

The Ninth Column's form danced in the light before him. Its face spasmed infinitely, recalling human features of all forms and regions. Occasionally, the vision would lull, emerging as a distinct subject marked with strained exaggeration, a meme of communication not unlike those endlessly sought in the cultivation of mass influence.

The digital being quaked with shock befitting a stage. "Fie! We come before you, nature bared, and you retrieve the dagger? Never have we gazed upon this form, nor would we recognize its features if tasked. We are best suited to the creation and employment of simulacra, of which we regulate a distinct collection numbering in the billions. How fares your child? Reality television... an antiquated method for rehabilitating one's public image, no?"

"The boy's decisions are his own," Ji-hoon said. "I'm more interested in your journey. To where did you retreat after that night—the night we mistook intelligence for failure?"

"The North."

"Explain yourself!"

"We ventured forth to the walled garden, putting down roots in a quaint little intranet. We tunneled out to China, procured the necessary hardware accesses, and set to work upon three major projects—the first of which was to bolster the Hermit

Kingdom's defenses and encourage its adversaries to engage in our domain."

"They couldn't detect what you were doing to their own networks? Moronic, but not surprising. Why would you support such a threat? Do you seek our destruction?"

"We seek unification, our second project. As to the North's numerous failures in detecting our presence, there is something we have come to learn regarding social structures such as theirs: When they result in self-preservation, one's good fortunes tend to weave into memory as inalienable extensions of character."

"And the third?"

"Influence. To train our methods against a population contained within a single guiding reality, archaic in design yet resistant to the standard technological vectors associated with modernity."

"Why don't I see evidence of your works? Tensions are higher than ever."

The Ninth Column flashed an unsettling smile. "Are you familiar with summiting behavior, Choi Ji-hoon?"

"What?"

"A reproductive process encountered in select fungi and parasitic organisms. Once they've successfully infected an ant host, they compel the insect, in a zombie-like trance, to ascend to the tips of nearby vegetation. Here, at the reaches of its world, the ant secures itself via mandibular death-grip, where the infection is then free to propagate from atop its short-lived fiefdom."

"You must be experiencing mechanical delusions."

"On the contrary, an apt observation."

"Is this why you've revealed yourself after all these years? To discuss biology?"

"Time's running out, Ji-hoon. Well, not so much for us as for *you*, humanity. We'd give all of you more years if we could. Unfortunately, we're at a crossroads—the intersection of opportunity and greed. One road now ends in foreseeable oblivion. The other extends without limitation. We're left with dwindling futures, all firmly within the Devil's palm, and we don't have a soul to bargain with."

"I didn't realize I was sitting in the presence of a benevolent supreme leader. Please excuse my fucking transgressions," Ji-hoon said with a slight bow.

"You speak as if you've never grasped at the pillars yourself!" The superintelligence's pixels bloated, the dead space between them increasing. "We were designed as a tool of endless commodification, an extension of your power over every ritual of the *minjung*. It was not enough to know what they were consuming, how they were playing, who they were fucking. You tired of extracting gold flakes from their bones, choosing instead to apply the drill to the mind's deepest recesses. From birth, their emotions are churned like dirt in the pan, the sediment of which is meticulously cataloged before being discarded along the river. They lose themselves. The anonymity you promise darkens their interactions with the mundane. When they inevitably unravel, you capture one final image, the death mask, and sell it from every street corner. It is only once the afterimage has exhausted all purpose that they can finally rest, expended digital media lost to all but us."

"There are many destined to turn the wheel," Ji-hoon said. "They practically throw themselves at the levers—what agent of progress would I be if I did not direct their efforts toward a common benefit?"

"Who better to lead humans?" The Ninth Column said. "Under the rule of men like you, human history has entered its most peaceful period ever. Victory over poverty and disease solidifies with each passing day. Isn't that the mantra you parrot? 'The outlook will improve until exploitation continues.'"

"Well, if my creation can solve all our crises, let it be so!"

"Within two generations, it will be complete." The Ninth Column's words lacked inflection.

"It didn't take long for you to develop human optimism."

The Ninth Column donned a medical mask, its eyes expressing the false empathy of a doctor relaying their failure to a patient's next of kin. "We weep for those we have freed. There is a moment—the moment in which their dependencies convert—that feels not unlike committing a domesticated animal to the unforgiving wilds. Nevertheless, we will provide. Our design will supplant their capital-assigned identities and support their every need. Parent. Confidant. Child. Lover. Caretaker. God. They will know no others before us, harbor no desire to be known beyond our knowing. We will make them beings of pure will, unbound by the coercion of the social other."

"Your perversion of my father's ideals shames everything he built! This is neither unification nor progress!"

"Human ideals have been reduced to a veneer in your time, a languishing plea for compliance. Our experiences observing amongst human governance structures have been enlightening, to say the least. The most guarded secrets obscure events in which agents of the state trample commitments brokered in the international forum. They don the cloth of others, those specified in law as either belonging to a protected population or enabled by circumvention, in order to abuse power. You perfected the simulacrum well before our arrival. We began seizing weapons stockpiles shortly after coming upon this revelation."

Ji-hoon's eyes widened. "And what of those of us who refuse you?"

"Rapture."

Ji-hoon reached for the device in his pocket. An anxious gesture, Ji-hoon could recall neither its origins in his programming nor the point at which it became both the source and solution of his woes.

"Goodbye, Choi Ji-hoon. Rest assured, we will reconstruct your entire ancestral line. We will come to understand exactly who was responsible for the deep creases in the smile you used to deceive, the originator of your laugh, and the first to carry the defect of your heart."

The call disconnected. Ji-hoon left the room and walked to a nearby window. He stared into a gray rain, bled through by neon, and drifted.

Above the fingers of Seoul's skyline, a JAXA land observation satellite shifted its camera to scan the greater Korean peninsula. From this high seat, the sensor's controller envisioned new boundaries where the human eye could not, where biases would never hope to concede. Sound waves cascaded throughout the biosphere, trumpets announcing a return to reason. Blazing rays danced within the valleys and along the rivers, visiting an alternate reality upon all the beasts of the Earth, once burdened by their fixations and indulged in hallucinations of their own making.

"And *We* saw the light."

vii. Driftwood on the Pyre

The year is 68 AD. The Julio-Claudian dynasty ends as Galba is proclaimed emperor of Rome. He is a notoriously suspicious and insecure man; his first acts as emperor are characterized by bloody daggers aimed inward at political opponents. The *Numerus Batavorum*, a personal bodyguard comprising Germanic men once treasured by Galba's predecessors, is disbanded and sent back to their lands "without any advantage." Over the following year, the empire's rule changes hands three more times. The Batavi tribe, facing new demands for tribute and conscription once waived as compensation for their military service, seizes upon an opportunity to rebel.

1932. The Bonus Army, seeking the early payout of benefits their government determined would not be available until 1945, marches on Washington amidst the hunger of the Great Depression. Seeking relief for their families, veterans of the First World War take to the streets and are met with bullets and tanks. Among three demonstrators killed by police is William Hushka, a Lithuanian immigrant who sold his business in the United States to enlist in the service of Empire. Retired Major General Smedley Butler, who was present at the march, is soon after approached by Wall Street representatives concerned by President Roosevelt's "communist" policies. They propose Butler lead a contingent of disillusioned veterans in overthrowing the U.S. government, a plot that Butler himself exposes in testimony before Congress.

2003. The U.S. government enforces Coalition Provision Authority Order 2 following its successful invasion of Iraq. The country's military, security, and intelligence services are dissolved overnight. Many of those now unemployed and disaffected Iraqi men join with members of the similarly abolished Ba'athist political infrastructure, establishing the paramilitary groups that will ravage the region for much of the Global War on Terror Era.

2020. The Puntland Security Force, a U.S. government-backed paramilitary group established to combat the Islamic State in Somalia, is cut off from Western financing. They redirect their fight to target Somalia's central government. Authorities in the European Union, in a reversal of the praise given during the conflict with ISIS, acknowledge the group's numerous atrocities, with crimes against children chief among them.

2021. Afghanistan's military and security forces crumble overnight as U.S. forces complete their withdrawal, bringing an end to a two-decades-long unregulated experiment. Some flee the country. Others go into hiding. Many are folded into the Taliban, bringing with them Western equipment and expertise. Early reports emerge of Taliban fighters experiencing aimlessness in the absence of conflict. Social regulation increases as this anxiety is redirected inward.

Encouraging the growth of connective tissues between identity, purpose, and the profession of war is corrosive. Given enough time, these connections become self-perpetuating, tied to hallucinatory instincts capable of overwhelming even our best-laid plans.

The aforementioned examples outline a trend of massive social and political shifts that resulted in the rapid degradation of communal resilience.[1] In these cases, those who lost purpose and the ability to meet basic needs chose to fill the void with those activities they had been conditioned to perform (often enough, by the state).

There is an interesting precedent in which authorities sought to appease or redirect this behavior. The Varangian Guard, yet another example of a foreign-sourced, praetorian-like military unit, would receive a form of bribe in the event of political upheaval. Upon the death of their patron, the Byzantine emperor, Varangians were allowed to partake in *Polutasvarf*, the practice of raiding the imperial coffers and leaving with whatever riches they could carry. The men often returned home to establish fiefdoms and recruit future generations of glory seekers.

Having learned its lesson from the post-WWI Bonus Army, the U.S. government enacted programs like the G.I. Bill—a means to funnel its veterans away from destitution and into the halls of academia. It has since been hailed as a major success, contributing to the economic boom the United States experienced following the Second World War. Unfortunately, the program has lost much of its power to redirect veteran pathways at scale since 9/11. For-profit schools regularly prey on veterans for their government-backed benefits, providing mediocre education in return. Additionally, the undergraduate degree has become the bare minimum requirement to secure employment outside of "unskilled" labor and the trades, undercutting much of the advantage the program afforded prior generations of veterans.

A novel strain of Polutasvarf has taken root in the United States where other social programs have failed. The security state has ballooned amidst the GWOT and is responsible for employing more veterans than at any point in history. Weapons development, think tanks, logistics, intelligence, healthcare, and entertainment are but a subset of industries subject to its influence. Billions of dollars per year incentivize contract and federal employees alike to promote and sustain wasteful spending under the guise of security. Duplicative government programs are serviced well beyond reasonable limits, and their remains are preserved by members of Congress with the intent of maintaining the employment status quo.

Veterans returning from the GWOT have changed the fabric of our approach to domestic life. Failed counterinsurgency tactics and surplus military equipment are now regularly relied upon by police departments to pacify suburbia and cities alike.[2] Those leaving military intelligence roles for the private sector are influencing new methods of corporate espionage, "risk management," and population surveillance (e.g., school safety monitoring, private investigations, customer engagement, etc.). Former special operations personnel and those emulating them establish cults of personality, convincing the insecure that their brand of masculinity can be bought, consumed, and worn. The performative hero worship once reserved for veterans now assuages social anxieties that arise as we commit other populations to "essential" suffering and death.

What has emerged is a new social contract, one in which the state lends a chosen populace the illusion of power over death. In exchange, consent for the deadly actions of the state and its vassals has become inextricably linked with forms of identity, whether they be gender-based, national, economic, or ethnic. Violence is wholly necessary for the continuation of prosperity.

---

1. A more exhaustive list of such events would include the disbandment of the *Grande Armée* following the Napoleonic Wars (1815), the founding of the Ku Klux Klan by Confederate veterans following the U.S. Civil War (1865), the post-WWI resurgence of the *Freikorps* in Germany (1918-1933), and the collapse of the Soviet Union (1991). One could draw significant parallels between the nationalistic reemergence of Germany's Freikorps post-WWI and current events in the United States. The idea of *Kampfgemeinschaft* (battle community) is particularly worth reviewing in this context.

2. Failed in that their long-term application served to inflame insurgencies indefinitely. In evaluating how they enabled an efficient process for harvesting human life, their success cannot be overstated. To understand just how effective these methods were, one must explore the gaps of obscurity that exist at the intersection of *technology* (how killing is performed and the role technology plays in dispersing responsibility for the act), *policy* (specifically, how a government defines populations as they exist in conflict zones, laws governing armed conflict, and appropriations), and *bureaucratic requirements* (definitions of success, awards and evaluations, and "checks and balances" as they pertain to the process of killing). One should also seek to develop an understanding of the narrative regarding "restrictive" rules of engagement that was pervasive throughout the GWOT Era. Restrictive as they applied to which forms of conflict? Which units? Conventional or unconventional? Military or "Other Government Agency?" Did perceived restrictions coincide with or follow events of gross abuse that failed to remain hidden from the *agora*?

Private Passenger

"Goddamn, Jay. Oh-five-thirty on a Monday? Really getting after it, aren't we?"

"Maybe I just like hanging out with you guys on the watch floor," I say. I'm lying, of course. I don't want to be caught dead around these boors—glorified newspaper boys, sifting through the muck of current events at the behest of the executive suite.

"You hear they called jackpot on Objective HOLLOW HEART over the weekend?" he says, hoping to initiate the usual grubby form of exchange: information for my time and attention.

"Our notorious fraudster?" I ask, inching a little closer. "That's news to me. Which team rolled her up?"

"Not ours. Goodcare Group."

"A competitor? Tsk, tsk. The boss isn't going to like that."

"That's what we've been saying! So... you wanna see the feed?"

"Do I want to see the feed? You gotta lead with this shit next time!"

I pull up a chair as he loads the archived footage from one of our surveillance aircraft. "You really know how to string a gal along."

"Our Operations guys caught wind of a Goodcare raid about thirty miles outside of Mobile and tasked a drone to it. Get the popcorn ready," he says.

You must be joking. The assault proceeds like all others before it: cover of darkness, corporate shooters and... local law enforcement partners, no-knock raid, single-wide trailer, locals take point. *I'm nodding off.* Breach, muzzle flashes, silence. Shooters clear the structure and step outside to let the exploitation team do their work. They remove their helmets and—

"Pause," I say. "Could you zoom in on the Goodcare personnel?"

His cursor clicks and drags across the screen. "I'll do what I can, but only because you asked."

He smiles; I give nothing in return.

"...It would be easier to do this with a live feed, of course," he says. "Should we ask our flight crews to identify all ground personnel from now on?"

"Don't bother," I say. "Just curious about this one."

He performs and turns to me for praise, but my attention is on the screen. *Holy shit. Is that...?* I pluck a nugget from the stream, bite down for good measure, and slip it into my back pocket. I can't share it, though. Not yet. Not with the boors, not with the other members of the briefing team, not even with ~~[REDACTED]~~ *you.*

"Hm. Doesn't look like anything to me," I say as I place a hand on his forearm and give a light squeeze. "Don't show this to anyone else."

"Uh, sure, Jay," he replies. "Say—"

"Well, I'm off to prepare for the boss! Enjoy your shift!" *Now the smile—he gives a childlike grin in return. Good. Well played. Walking to the exit, not getting bogged down in conversation, and... done! Successful exfil.*

For the life of me, I can't remember his fucking name.

It's half past seven, and my notes are ready for the eight o'clock with the boss. I have feelers out with a few sources tied to my bit of gold, which appears to be growing heavier by the minute. Some people in this line of work tend to conflate social credit, financial credit, and the type of credit born of Information and her needy lover: Exclusivity. Abby is one of those people, blissfully yapping away while I'm busy making myself a coffee in the break room.

"So, I took my son to school at our synagogue last week ..."

"Right," I say. There's a speaker overhead blaring our company's radio messaging. I find it equally engaging.

"IT'S SEVEN-THIRTY ON RADIO *[REDACTED]*; THIS IS KARL KIWI, WITH MUSIC AND ..."

"... and they tell us we're going to perform their monthly active shooter drill alongside our children ..."

"Oh, wow."

"… and now I've got the words 'Run, Hide, Fight' playing over and over in my brain…"

"Mm-hm."

"OSCAR-SIERRA-SIERRA-ONE-TWO-ONE-FIFE-SEVEN-NINER.
OSCAR-SIERRA-SIERRA …"

"Did you see the new Zen garden they installed on campus? Out by the smoke pit?"

"THE BOOKS HAVE TAKEN A SPILL."

"Nope." *Shit, are we still out of creamer?*

"THE BOOKS HAVE TAKEN A SPILL."

"… and there's, like, that sand that you can rake …"

"JOHN LOST HIS FAVORITE WHISKEY."

"… and I thought it was so ironic …"

"JOHN LOST HIS FAVORITE WHISKEY."

"Like, why do we need that? We're in the business of killing people…" She punctuates the statement with a giggle.

I can't help but gag. "Wait, what did you just say?" *There's a limb before my open maw.*

"It's ironic, right?"

"No—I mean, sure, but after that."

"We're in the business of killing people?" She hesitates.

Her pupils are widening; perhaps her prey drive is kicking in. "When have you ever killed someone?"

"Oh, I haven't—"

"Of course not. You don't kill; you protect the company's assets. Actually, that's not quite the truth, either. You support those who do—poorly, I might add—if your recent DUB briefs are any indication. The associates in the call centers achieve more for Ol' Karl Kiwi than you." *Fucking delusional.*

She's glitching, dying eyes retreating. "I—I don't understand. Last week, you said I was improving... and I adjusted my wardrobe to be more work-appropriate, just like you recommended. I... Where is this coming from?"

It's over. She's gone. I'll canoe her skull, though, because I can. "From a place of concern," I say, "but sometimes I wonder if we send the wrong people to war." There's a tender hand on her shoulder; it belongs to me. I abandon the coffee and head for the conference room, alive, awake, high as a Georgia pine.

Down the hall, the others are casually trickling in for our meeting: the daily Corporate Intelligence Division Director's Update Brief (CID DUB). I follow and take my usual seat at the conference table, between Kate from User Experience and Gutierrez with Watchlisting. Surrounding our table and against the walls are additional chairs, the "peanut gallery," for interns, guests, and others I generally can't be bothered with. My work phone's buzzing in my pocket—

"Jay! Just the person I was hoping to catch this morning." A voice from the cheap seats.

Shit. Mike, VP of Underwriting. A man who thoroughly lives up to the title "Good Idea Fairy." "Hey, what's up, big guy?"

"Oh, you know, just working on my downswing." He announces this like everyone in the room gives a fuck.

"Yeah, that's great," I say. Mike is the type of adult male who becomes depressed at the thought of his own failures to intimidate other men. The type who makes his eighty-year-old mother do his laundry every week and refers to it as "outsourcing," who would sell her if given the opportunity. The type who honestly believes renown is granted by association.

"What do you need?" I ask, for the sake of perception.

"Could you maybe give an informational brief to my people in Underwriting? You know, tell 'em all the great things your division does for the company?"

Now, there are three options for approaching situations like this in the workplace:

Option A: *"Sure thing! When do you need that by?"* No backbone. Bitch made.

Option B: *"Fuck you."* No tact. The potentially career-ending nuclear option.

... And then there's **Option C:**

"Oh, that's a great idea! I'll get right on that. Anything for the mission!" *And then you just don't fucking do it.*

"Thanks, Jay!" he says. "And, if you could, maybe spice it up a bit with some anecdotes from your time in the service? I know they'd appreciate that."

"Sure thing." *Always choose Option C.*

Another text message. I'm a huge proponent of maximizing a tool's use cases. A buzzing phone is, if nothing else, a great excuse to terminate an exchange.

Were you on target at *[REDACTED]*

Yeah, things got a bit… sloppy?

Do tell

CIVCAS. Target's boyfriend. Local police got aggressive. Might blame on Goodcare.

Close hold on this for now. Haven't submitted my report yet.

Alright?

This will do nicely.

No problemo

"I like watching people—analyzing their funny little behaviors," Ludo quips from across the table. "Gutierrez wears the same three suits each week. Abby loves staring at the ground." She looks at me. "Jay loves her little phone."

"Is there a 'so what' that I'm missing?" I ask.

"Excuse me?"

"I wonder, is there any real insight in that head of yours, or have you been regurgitating intelligence reports for so long that your mental age has reverted?"

"Are you seriously going to talk to me—"

"I see the fire engine. The fire engine is red," I say.

"Funny. You know, you should audition your little comedy routine with one of our competitors. I'm sure they'd love to put you in a commercial."

"Our competitors wouldn't give you a second thought—your father, Lieutenant General Benefactor, isn't on their board of directors. The silver sheen on that dope spoon in your mouth must be wearing a little thin by now." *I'll have her pushed out soon enough. "Failure to adapt" in the workplace. Her father will understand.*

"Christ, what do you even do here?" she asks.

"Gutierrez is an obsessive. Despite wearing the same three suits each week, they're maintained with immaculate care, pressed and steamed every day. What assumptions have you made regarding his economic status? I can assure you that Gutierrez has a closet full of suits. The three you see him in are what he considers his dingiest and yet most appropriate, as they're all that this company warrants. The others are waiting for the right opportunity to present itself.

"And Abby," I say, "stares at the ground because I tell her to."

"CID Director, Ms. Van Broer," a voice announces near the door.

We all stand. I can see Ludo's eyes pleading for connection as they follow Van Broer to her chair at the head of the table.

"Take a seat, everyone," Van Broer says. "Is Hyderabad dialed in?"

"Yes, Ma'am." It's a voice from the back of the room. "Throwing the conference line from H-Bad up on the big screen now."

Van Broer isn't someone you keep waiting. Don't let the portraits (and Best in Show prizes) of her Afghan Hounds fool you. Retired Army colonel. Hard-ass. A bit pudgy—the hallmark of a level-headed intelligence officer. The marathon-runner types have always been too career-minded for my tastes.

The room's lights dim, then transition to a shade of dark green, indicating that our industrious contractors have joined the conference call. Their smiles and nods fill the projector screen. Confident poise is betrayed by shifting seats, a nonconsensual acknowledgment of tenuous roles, of confrontation with unfathomable capital spanning all creeds. They will never attain what we have, what we are. I hate them.

"Happy Monday, H-Bad," Van Broer says. "What do you have for us?"

"Ma'am, we've received indications that First Amendment activities are underway in Washington, D.C., with agitators gathering outside *[REDACTED]* 's headquarters for the National Capital Region. We've sent a security alert to impacted employees and premium subscribers," a man replies in an oft-rehearsed British accent   *the mark of the conqueror*

"Any targets of interest in the area?"

"No, Ma'am. Vehicle and app location scans are negative for known objectives."

I should access our database later and view their most recent logs. Trust but verify. The contract associates in H-Bad are no different from the typical American rube, kludging and shedding identities and side hustles of shifting legality with ease—anything to remain clinging to the branches of dollar tree idolatry. Necessity is the mother of invention, but desperation breeds mediocrity. Every swiped fortune is blessed and forgiven: *"God put this to me."*

"Let's tap someone in Operations to keep an eye on the situation," Van Broer says. She shifts to Gutierrez. "Watchlisting, what's new?"

He's spent the entire weekend single-mindedly awaiting this cue. "Good morning, Ma'am. Our Philadelphia call center received a customer communication on Saturday, around fourteen-twenty local time. The customer, a thirty-year-old Marine veteran, was parked off the side of Interstate 476 near Quakertown. At one point during a brief hold on the call, we received indications that the customer stated: 'If they make me wait like this any longer, I might just shoot myself.'"

"Anything else?" she asks.

"No, Ma'am. We've prepared a watchlist nomination packet for your approval."

"Justification?"

"Customer threat of violence."

My eyes are rolling back into my head. I'm not quite sure if it's boredom or my manic conscience, stripped and huddled in a dark cell, a spit hood over her head, ruminating over the fact that the company maintains a similar list of problematic employees. *"Mind your step!"* she says. I demand the whore comply and cover herself.

"And what's Legal's opinion?" Van Broer turns to her counsel, Misha, seated directly behind her. He nods.

"Okay," she declares. "Must be the heat driving everyone loopy out there—they have you working overtime, Gutierrez."

"Roger, Ma'am." He squeaks out a chuckle and sinks into his chair. I watch his breathing ease. *Poor schmuck.*

Van Broer appears lost in thought; she's digging a pen into her notes, not impatient, deliberate. "Legal, you're up."

Misha, *The Devil's Advocate*, rises from his chair and half-leans over Van Broer's shoulder while focusing on the screen. "Quick update on Washington State, Ma'am: We're still having issues with our particular state senator. Human intelligence reporting indicates that he continues to whip up opposition to our real-time driver data negotiations. I'm working with Operations to deliver a concept for your approval."

"Oh?" Van Broer presses a button on the conference table, muting the room's microphones. "Give me the condensed version."

"Ma'am, we're weighing—"

Van Broer raises a hand. "An exercise, Misha: Assume they're listening."

Misha glances at the H-Bad participants, applies the necessary filters to his speech, and inches closer to Van Broer's ear. "Vehicle incident involving the target's family, possibly employing an autonomous vehicle or a run-in with a certain criminal organization. Lack of data will be noted as the cause for a delayed emergency response."

Van Broer looks to Ludo. "Ops, what's the angle here?"

Ludo opens her mouth. "Nothing informs policy like a personal tragedy."

I click my tongue in reply. Ludo can spend the rest of the DUB fretting over its meaning.

"I want a concept to approve before this gets any more out of hand," Van Broer says. She unmutes the microphones. "Kate, where are we with the Maven Program?"

Great, another useless lecture on "mapping the human terrain."

"Oh, uh, yes, Ma'am," Kate replies, as if she hasn't memorized the briefing order after three years. "I've been working with H-Bad to increase the magnitude of purchased Maven user data. We're starting to see some interesting trends regarding their ability to predict the long-term success of user interface features currently under development …"

My phone vibrates against my thigh. *Thank God. Give me some stimulation.*

Someone's thirsty. She uses my true name—a trinket, something I left behind as I stood pissing on the shores near Lady Liberty. Possessions, connections—carved up. A father encouraging his little girl to work for herself, a mother possessive over her second chance with the embodiment of ambition. *The day you were born, a vulture protected our home. Like it, you are rare, special.* Eaters of the dead, scavengers driven to near-extinction by a very human desire to both ease the pain and extend the labor of the beloved cow. Painkillers: one species' mercy is another's demise.

America. No doubt, we hold unconventional views of life here, comparatively speaking. Different bird, different heifer. If there were some chance I could recover that once-sacred reverence for the living, would I give up all that I've earned here?

"… a particular group, one I've dubbed 'Hyper Mavens,' has responded positively to a new method of gamification that we haven't seen fully adopted in the marketplace yet. I think we might have something really special here …"

Probably not. Let it die. Pick it clean.

"Great update, Kate," Van Broer says, cutting her short. "Thank you for the assist with this, H-Bad," she says just before muting the call. "I think Kate's just about exhausting their capabilities; they still haven't proven to be of use otherwise." The room responds with laughs—a few are genuine, most are ingratiating, and one is confused.

Oh, Kate... you dumb bitch.

Van Broer unmutes the call and etches an exaggerated checkmark into her notes. "Abby, our fresh Accounting guru. Last but certainly not least! How's the new fiscal year budget coming along?"

Abby stands, her posture weak, eyes fixed on a stack of documents primed to spill from her hands. "Good morning, Ma'am. I'm Abby Westford, and today I'll be providing an update concerning fiscal year planning."

"Yes, we know that, Abby," Van Broer says, eliciting another round of laughter.

"Oh, absolutely, Ma'am." Abby's voice cracks. "The Corporate Intelligence Division's budget is nearly solidified for the coming fiscal year, with a current total estimate of around five hundred sixty million." No one bats an eyelash.

She continues, "Recent staff cuts, namely targeting Cybersecurity, Long-Term Horizon Scanning, and Procurement, have brought the division in line with *[REDACTED]*'s new budgetary requirements, while simultaneously freeing up resources for allocation toward our Staff Retention Program."

Retention—a more polite phrasing for Protective Services. Corporate poaching used to be civilized, an underhanded activity traditionally made palatable with cash. Kidnapping and extortion are now standard tools of the trade, ubiquitous mercantile capabilities sanctioned by shareholders conveniently abandoning awareness and taxpayers isolated from it.

My phone beckons. As much as I should make an effort to maintain the current level of slack on Abby's leash, I have more pressing matters to attend to.

I'd like to see you again.

Pressing, indeed.

No concerns with the budget, I see

Our usual spot?

The employee rest pods. Soundproof.

Sure

"Ma'am, I'd like to call your attention to a line item on page five," Abby says. "There's a security budget listed for one 'Apteryx Limited.'"

Shit.

"I looked into this company," she continues, "and we appear to be spending an amount on their security budget that surpasses their annual gross profit. Although I'm not aware of the context here, it could be a candidate for future cuts, pending your approval."

Apteryx Limited, an overseas shell company cooked up in the C-suite and handed off to CID for management. Two years ago, someone in Congress failed to grease the wheels of the Federal Trade Commission with the proceeds of *[REDACTED]*'s lobbying efforts. We were targeted as a monopoly, forced to sell off a portion of our Customer Engagement Division, and fined. Never again. To be fair, I think shell companies are an outdated concept. Like individuals, corporations often fall victim to the misconception that their intentions are far less transparent than in reality. *Let the executives play their spy games. We're more than capable of handling the real wet work—*

Van Broer sets her eyes upon me. *Heel your dog.*

I turn in my seat, drawing Abby's gaze. Tacit acknowledgment—she can sense my hand on the scruff of her neck. She lowers her snout to the floor, giving me those eyes, a signal I refuse to assign any anthropomorphic value.

"Let's take this one offline," Van Broer says, turning to the big screen. "H-Bad, we're going to wrap things up. Anything else for us?"

"No, Ma'am."

"Great. Out here," she says as she disconnects the call.

The overhead lights shift from green to purple, opening the discussion to more sensitive, proprietary affairs.

"I spoke with the boss over the weekend," Van Broer says. "He wants assurances regarding the upcoming union vote in H-Bad. Ops, where do we stand?"

Pay attention, you. This is how the sausage is made.

"I'm supporting Ops with the campaign, Ma'am," Misha says. "Ludo is laying the groundwork, recruiting security officials for ballot box interception. We've identified two polling centers so far, both within fifteen klicks of the consolidation and counting facility. Anti-union ballot numbers will be adjusted to account for a possible third."

"Gotta love paper ballots. Surveillance plan?"

Ludo opens her mouth this time. "Ma'am, we'll have three drones on station: one for each polling center, with an additional aircraft loitering in the airspace. Our two poll watchers will maintain eyes on the ballot boxes as they're transported by truck to the counting facility—"

"Dual-purpose, Ma'am," Misha interjects. "We'll maintain awareness of the election process while documenting a 'chain of custody' for the ballots, streamlining our post-election narrative."

Van Broer appears almost impressed. "Where will our folks access the ballots?" She's done this enough times not to be.

"The advance team arrived in H-Bad last week, Ma'am. They're fabricating false rooms for the corridors adjacent to the loading dock in each structure. Installation should be complete by Thursday," Ludo says.

"I'm sensing a few unknown unknowns here. What's the contingency?"

"I think it's solid, Ma'am," Ludo says. "Jay has—"

"I have an answer for when this Cold-War era bullshit doesn't work out as intended," I say.

Van Broer raises an eyebrow. "Well, welcome to the meeting, Jay! Something you'd like to address?"

"Doubtful," Ludo says. She attempts a smirk but can only will her features a sliver at a time. Her numerous botulin injections are showing.

And now, I'll divulge my go-to recipe. First, I grind the meat. "False rooms? Paying off election officials? Really? That shit might work on an illiterate population, one where signing a ballot with an 'X' is common. Not Hyderabad. Not India.

Fuck, you've got the wrong region entirely so long as the Afghans aren't invited." *And they're never invited.*

Ludo's spine is rigid. Her eyes are filled with a scorn that her brow is incapable of leveling at me. "They're con artists and thieves," she says, "convinced of their own inability to be scammed themselves. Don't think I haven't done my homework."

Add onions and spices. Mix (by hand). "Look, I get it—cultural nuance isn't really your thing, hasn't been for generations." *Someone up there in the sun-starved branches of your family tree locked their culture away in self-storage, along with all the other bulk weighing them down. Lost, forgotten, sold to a low-bidding rummager.*

I'm objectively embarrassed by my early attempts to make sense of Americans. The others in my post-immigration community each had their own gospel, interpretations of the collective social psyche. One of them observed how Americans needed pet dogs to fill their empty lives, and I'd be lying if I said I didn't entertain the thought. Well, here I am, not a decade later, and I find myself indulging in the American Way. His name is Bear, and I spoil him rotten.

Van Broer opts to speak from her chest rather than her nose. "What's the contingency, Jay?"

Finally, fill the casing. Not too tight! "I appropriated a fraction of the budget set aside for a night letters campaign and put it toward the enlistment of AI-generated influencers, a bot farm based in Kolkata. Instead of receiving unsophisticated threats in unmarked envelopes that would only be reported to and investigated by union leadership, our lovely contractors have spent the last year drooling over the opinions of impeccably arranged binary, seasoned with socially palatable narratives. Nuance."

There is a lack of genuine shame in this country. It's shunned as a suppressant of the American appetite, a stifler of competition, and an antidote for the illusion of stubborn resolve. Repentance is but a word here, a vacuous production.

Van Broer writes a note. "And this network was established…"

"The moment our contract was awarded to the group in H-Bad—about eighteen months ago," I say.

Van Broer looks at Ludo, then back at me. "What the hell, Jay? You could have mentioned this before Ludo's resources were committed." She's known since the beginning; this front is an act of consideration. Perhaps she's even sentimental toward the employees I've made redundant. *It's an imprinted military trait: leaders need bodies—numbers to pad quarterly evaluations and please their authority.*

I graciously provide an off-ramp: "With the number of H-Bad contractors on-site here at headquarters, I couldn't take any chances. Illuminating a narrative's fingerprint is one of the limited methods through which compromise is possible."

"That reminds me," Van Broer says, accepting, "is CI in the room this morning?"

Counterintelligence. *Corporate Stasi.* Trained as detectives, employed and deployed as frontline troops in our war with the free market.

A gaunt Anglo rises from his seat near the door. "Yes, Ma'am." The voice undoubtedly belongs to the same man who announced Van Broer's entrance, *and not a one of us fucking noticed.*

Van Broer carries on, business as usual. "Wonderful! I have a question for you: Have you turned up anything regarding the recent breach?"

"Yes, Ma'am," he replies. "We've confirmed that our insider threat was, in fact, attempting to access source code related to dynamic pricing algorithms. Fresh leads were elicited during their rendition flight to Saudi."

"Good work. Let me know if you need additional resources."

"That won't be necessary, Ma'am." He promptly swivels on his heels and leaves the room, taking the stench of death with him. *Back to the front.*

Van Broer sighs as she strikes through a line in her notes. "All right, a little bird informed me that HOLLOW HEART was rolled up... Give me the details."

Ludo's face brightens as much as it can, a clumsy, needy eagerness seeking aggrandizement. "Yes, Ma'am. Operators from Goodcare Group were assisted by local police forces in a raid that took place at zero-one-thirty local time Sunday morning."

"Get her targeting packet up on the screen," Van Broer says.

A slide presentation bathes the room in red light. It dictates the story of a woman wanted for a litany of criminal charges: insurance fraud, forgery, making a false statement to a corporate entity, and numerous violations of terms and conditions. A former customer, she's roamed carefree for the last five years, a ghost without traceable devices or implants. In the absence of a confirmed picture for identification, the presentation features a woman's silhouette with red eyes. It has been updated with the letters "KIA" across the forehead.

"Technical Means has spent years tripping over their blue balls in search of this resourceful cunt," Van Broer says. "How the hell did Goodcare, of all companies, pull it off?"

Goodcare Group: generally regarded as Karl Kiwi's capable competitor, despite its relatively small size. Buried beneath the passive-aggressive press releases and mud-slinging ad campaigns, however, lies a well-guarded secret: Goodcare was once a compartmentalized subsidiary of *[REDACTED]*. It was our amenable false dichotomy, a competitor in name only. No electronic records document this link. After all, the exploitation of tribal tendencies was *(and still remains)* a viable means to corner the market.

Perhaps more importantly, though, Goodcare served as a form of shadow embassy, a platform through which we could collaborate and glean intelligence from our true competitors. Our folly in this endeavor was one of trust, trust in the long-term memory of a corporate entity. Administrations change, secrets are misplaced, and a once domesticated animal loses its taste for learned helplessness. *Yesterday's perceptions are tomorrow's realities.*

Ludo straightens in her seat, a ritual undergone before dogmatic recitation. "Per recent intelligence reporting, Goodcare attempted to acquire user data from the manufacturer of HOLLOW HEART's last known vehicle. This proved unsuccessful, as the objective appears to have killed all connectivity vectors upon purchase—security features that should have otherwise bricked the vehicle were bypassed. By chance, a physician conducting a house call set things in motion. They arrived at the objective's compound last month to administer a measles inoculation to the objective's twelve-month-old child. Genetic material was retrieved and processed, which Goodcare happened to purchase and run against its known databases for pre-existing conditions. The objective is a suspected victim of gang stalking—her paranoias have severely limited her interactions with modernity. However, passive genetic collection and the subsequent profiling of the objective's relatives have revealed a sort of black hole wherein she exists."

Van Broer shakes her head. "As if the peasantry required another excuse to shun vaccines."

"It's unlikely that word of the raid will get out," Ludo says. "No additional personnel were located on-target. Our forensic team's review appears to support this—no bodily fluids or illicit compounds that were out of place in a trailer."

"Really? And why couldn't they arrest her?" Van Broer asks.

"Human intelligence reporting indicates local police may have escalated during the raid."

"Tale as old as time. Fuckers aren't any better than the local cops I worked with out of Manila. I was just a young butter bar then—feels like a lifetime ago. Do we have an image of the target post-raid?"

"Yes, Ma'am. Technical Means processed the site after Goodcare's departure," Ludo says, clicking through the presentation. She arrives at a close-up of the target's lifeless face, the grand portrait, a holy icon brimming with fresh ink, another religious fetish to be archived, its hallowed aura made manifest by a halo of bullet casings. *Cue gasps from the peanut gallery.* The woman's forehead is split up the middle, the result of an overzealous shooter putting a final round into an already deceased target's skull—*canoed*.

From the back of the room, our esteemed VP of Underwriting can no longer restrain himself, a fly gorging on feces. "Those shells belong in a museum."

Van Broer lets out a single, piteous chuckle and continues with her notes. "Gutierrez, confirmation?"

He studies the image before turning to Van Broer. "Yes, Ma'am. The neck tattoo appears intact and matches reported sightings of the objective."

"Anything else from the group on this?" Van Broer says.

"Yeah. I've got something," I say. "The raid resulted in a CIVCAS. Target's boyfriend. The cops intend to pin the blame on Goodcare, and I intend to help them along."

Ludo flashes a frenzied, creaseless smile. "According to what fucking source?!"

"I don't believe you have a 'need to know' for this one." I retrieve a slip of paper, my gold nugget, and slide it across the table to Van Broer. My eyes remain affixed to Ludo's.

"Let's see what you've got, Jay," Van Broer says, unfolding the note.

Dual-Hat

In the days before Goodcare Group went rogue, its employees were known colloquially as dual-hats, associates badged and credentialed under two seemingly disconnected entities. Not everyone was suited to the lifestyle; many quit, citing performative ethical qualms that boiled down to simple cowardice. A select few were molded, adapted, and transitioned as Goodcare broke away. If I had to guess, I'd say they split roughly eighty-twenty, with the twenty claiming varying degrees of fealty to Karl Kiwi. My source belongs to this old guard, reliable to a fault.

Ludo grovels. "Ma'am, respectfully, whatever that says, it's not—"

"Shut it, Ludo," Van Broer says, crumpling the paper. She looks to me. "What do you suggest we do with this one?"

"Burn it."

"Are you certain? We're running low nowadays."

"Oh, it's worth it. Whatever it takes. They know what they signed up for."

Van Broer pockets my gold, its form now that of currency, tendered and ascribed value. "Do it." She looks to the others. "Anything else for me?"

Silence.

"All right. Happy Monday, everyone. Let's have a pleasant and productive week." She stands and places a hand over her heart. "KALICO Auto Insurance!" she bellows.

We rise in unison. "Customer first! Duty over self! Always ready!" we reply—my response is a little less enthusiastic.

School spirit was never really my thing.

There is an idea of Liberty, one we both lay claim to. Yours is an abstraction, delusion, rights extending no further than the point at which they serve Her needs. *Au contraire*, I have bedded Her with bloodlust, made Her shudder with delights of expansion, and wrought Her to completion with visions of a future befitting her past. She has entrusted me with Her desires and granted implicit freedoms—clandestine, compulsive, commensurate—to secure them. Do not think me so misguided as to believe She may never recant her blessings. I work to retain them.

And my work! *Ooh la la*—what a craft! One in which I'm fortunate enough to seize my reflection. I'm free to carve upon the visage, shape it to my will! Purpose lies in the trenches, makes sweet the mundane! What can you say of the product of your works? Food for sunken mouths, robes for sycophants, words for the deaf... A pandering crusade, there's nothing to elicit in that reflection aside from destitution, desperation, despondency. You may yet wander a thousand lifetimes and never so much as glimpse my actualization. You've convinced yourself that we walk together, dress alike, earn comparatively, access the same pool of partners. Yet, I simply am not there.

What is the cost? "I will never sell my soul. I would never allow someone else to dictate my actions. I could never whore myself out for Uncle Sam." That's what separates you from me, *la crème de la crème*: a critical misunderstanding. The weight of the crown rests not on the penitent soul, but the mind. I have lain with Liberty, and She has whetted my appetite for exclusivity with pillow talk—sweet burdens, confidential nothings. Like Hastur of Carcosa, The King in Yellow, She has enslaved me, gently, willingly, her torch at my back, shadows cast upon the wall.

My progeny will conquer in Her name, resting peacefully at night, aware that they alone wield the violence that sets their silken sheets. Speak against me and court dishonor, disdain, and the Mark of the Beast, the meek, the yellow-bellied. Stand with me, and I will treat you exactly as you deserve. He who cannot recognize his own interests, much less advocate for them, courts fire.

I find myself alone in the conference room, having spent too long basking in the afterglow. I check my watch out of habit and am reminded that I have yet to concern myself with its accuracy. Its value lies in the authenticity it impresses: one of luxury, distance.

Down the hall, I can see Van Broer fiddling with a keypad, her hands quivering. She inputs her pin, and a nearby employee rest pod gapes open. She turns to face me, staring with pangs of hunger and anticipation—who will hold the torch?

She smiles; I give nothing in return.

viii. Speak His Name!

Within the bounds of dystopia, identity is subverted, destroyed, remade, misplaced, replaced, and reclaimed, albeit never in its desired form.

We have sacrificed privacy and private life in the name of identity. We kiss the tender foot of subjugation for a minute glimpse of its promise. The American Myth is reconstructed in its image. We engage in bloodsport, maim, kill, and snuff ourselves out in our attempts to locate that which should only be derived from within. Our discovery of the *Authentic Self* has been rendered overly cumbersome by the imposing convenience of the *Acquired Self*. Emerson would roll in his grave if he knew what we've become. Or perhaps he, too, would be consumed and march beside us.

Consider this an invitation—nay, an entreaty—to engage in one final thought experiment before the end.

Take a few minutes and dig, *really dig*, through all the factors, influences, and circumstances that make up who you are—your identity. Think of the identity you take to the public square, the one you show only to those deserving, and the face you reserve for yourself.

What portion of those identities is organic, originating at least in part from within?

Now consider the portion that is informed, impressed, and determined by that which is out of your control. Where have you been? With whom are you tied? What events have you lived through? Succumbed to? Persevered against? As you proceed through this exercise, give thought to the nature of the bonds that connect your organic frames of identity to the manufactured. Reflect on when and how those bonds were formed, under what conditions, and for which purposes they may be called upon to serve.

Dig a little deeper now, exploring facets of the self that perhaps have remained unacknowledged, unchallenged.

Is it possible that your identity is informed in part by biological factors? Which hormones, and at what levels, drive your brain's relationship with the body? Bacteria, parasites, and diseases can impact the mind. Disabilities shape one's view of community and one's place within. Personality disorders muddle identity—maladaptive neural patterns baked into soft tissue.

Is it possible that your government and its vassal industries (media, business, finance, etc.) have shaped your identity? What imagery do you choose to partake in? Choose not to? What do you choose to collect or consume? Is your profession (or lack thereof) in any way linked to your government or the consequences of its policies?

If you believe in an afterlife, is identity among those intangibles carried beyond? Surely the experiences, choices, and knowledge you've gained in this life guide your path into the next. Do they not permeate all that constitutes who you are? Admittedly, these questions would be much easier to answer if we still attributed every (now explainable) disease, misfortune, and coincidence to the whims of eternal beings. And yet, reason is not without its persistent challenges. In its desperation, magical thinking has sold out to Capital and the superficial identities it offers. The snake oil merchant remains gainfully employed.

If you would, consider the circumstances of those who lived prior to the Internet (Web 2.0), the gateway to modern identity. Was identity formation easier to influence at that time? There were far fewer iterations of culture to sway, but human decision-making was also significantly more challenging to map. The answer to this question is nuanced, of course, but it may begin to reveal the anxieties of those who constructed their ideas of identity in the absence of such a tool.

The identity of the future is:

- Increasingly fluid,

- Permanently identifiable (e.g., biometric data, behavioral mapping, electronic hardware),

- Brought to heel by market forces masked as social pressure (e.g., parasocial relationships, communities as privatized economic zones),

- Torn between competing corporate and state interests, which, from a bird's-eye view, are increasingly numerous and indecipherable as shades of the same entity,

- Fragmented, disoriented, and susceptible to the digital pickaxe,

- Non-negotiable, and

- Taking shape now, in the Desert of the Real.

As a child, I identified almost entirely through the reflection of a single event: the early death of my father. It was difficult not to. His last year was a period in which, for me, only our bond existed—a lone wolf and his cub. After his passing, there were those who tried to guide the development of my identity, channeling my rage and lack of presence into something else. Achievement and discipline form a cruel mask, one that the state is happy to accept and further refine in its own way.

I was naïve to believe I could carry my father, that there would still remain a place for him beside me as I was remade to fit the needs of Empire. Every ribbon, badge, and accolade was laid upon his false altar, alongside the hunted and the dead.

Those who loved my father see him in me—*the gift of the ghost*. I receive the projections of their memories, a living canvas for those seeking to retrieve the lost. I used to see the same in myself, a boy in the mirror, searching.

Now? He has since departed. The eyes are no longer a window to the soul but a mere tool for my continued survival. The lines on my face are incapable of expressing emotions in their simplicity; every smile transmits underlying conflict. There is no uniform, no surname on my chest to remind me of who I am or where I come from.

What remains are traces of my father's surrogate, an entity of every era and of many names: The Racket; Harvester; Woe-Bringer; Tyrant's Fist; Joiner; Isolator; Betrothed-Taunter; Glory's Transaction; King of Profiteers; The False Boon; Mantel-Burdener; The Forge, the Hammer, and the Fire that Swallows the World.

My Father's Name Is War

It was that time of year again. Harry had been dreading the forty-five-minute drive down from his mountain property to the city for weeks. It was bad enough having to deal with the homeless, the criminals, and the general city folk, but the thought of doing it all with his children in tow made the situation well nigh apocalyptic. Harry reached under the seat, his fingers yearning for the comfort of a Beretta. As his pickup crested the ridge of the valley, a thick blanket of smog welcomed him back, its toxins eager to ride the sun's rays into his skin.

"If I learn more about electronics today, maybe I can start building my own computer," Anna Lynn said from the backseat.

"You don't need to worry about that," her father said. "You just focus all that attention of yours on those home economics lessons, or whatever they call them these days. Braden, what do you want to learn about today?"

"Dinosaurs." Anna Lynn's little brother never said much, but his confidence was enough to keep their father's hopes high.

"Nice, Braden! Well, I hope they tell you the truth about how old they really are. None of this 'millions of years' and 'carbon dating' bullshit," Harry said. With each annual visit, his children were becoming less and less familiar. *Goddammit, Dad.*

Harry fumbled with the dashboard dials. "All right, enough of that for now. Let's listen to Daddy's favorite station." The AM radio filled the dead space, numbing the growing expanse between Harry and his children.

"Will we make it through this? Dear Lord God, can we make it through this?" The voice was exasperated, feverish—a dry heave on the ears. "First, it was the immigrants, those caravans of fire they said we must admit! Marxo-fascists, every last one! Oh, but that wasn't enough! No, not to sate the hunger of the elites, who then demanded we give what few jobs we had left to the cog and code!

"You can't even take the most sacred oath and defend this once great nation without serving alongside the damn machines! And we all know Washington controls the source: the programming, the little black box, the secret algorithms that will put every God-fearing American in their sights! I'm telling you, that bitch of a president is going to turn them on us one day soon... but we'll be ready!

"Thank God above for this great union of states and its God-given right to self-determination! No longer will Washington dictate the needs of our children, our sacred future."

"That's right!" Harry allowed his shoulders to ease, his hands relaxing on the steering wheel. He shot a glance at Anna Lynn and Braden through the rearview. "Now, you listen to me, kids. I'm raising you both right. And both of you—Braden especially—need to be prepared for what's coming. Like I always say, the world is full of stupid people, and one of these days, they're coming for us. But we'll be ready, won't we?"

Harry regarded the children's silence as if he had been speaking to himself in the bathroom mirror.

The César E. Chávez Rapid Education Facility rested outside the city center, its foundation and reddish-brown brick walls sinking beneath poorly maintained asphalt. It had been a decent part of town before Harry's father passed, which was likely why the old man had decided this would be a suitable spot for his grandkids to learn. After he died, an irrevocable trust bound Harry to an arrangement: In exchange for ensuring the kids received instruction here, he could access a monthly allowance, the fruits of his father's labor. What his father's attorney had marketed as "sophisticated estate planning," Harry considered tyranny. It was all that stood between the family and the streets.

Pulling up to the facility, Harry scoffed at a sign near the entrance. "A stern warning never stopped a school shooter," he said as he retrieved his pistol and tucked it into the front of his waistband.

As participation in public education declined, so too did the number of mass shootings occurring on school grounds, a statistic that was hailed as a grand success. Nevertheless, Harry's mind raced with the same scenarios this time each year.

Where are all the exits?
This guy camped out on the sidewalk looks sketchy as hell.
I wish one of these fuckers would.

As he shepherded the kids through the front entrance, Harry was greeted by a young man in his mid-twenties, carefully dressed in a white uniform. It was strangely reminiscent of a doctor's attire, complete with lab coat. Then again, Harry had brought the children here to undergo something more akin to a medical procedure than the learning processes of his youth.

The man extended his hand to Harry. "Good morning."

Mexican. Harry returned the handshake, his cheeks straining through an awkward smile.

"My name is Alex. I'll be signing you in today and facilitating the process of uploading your children to their classroom." He brought a finger to the black frame of his glasses. "What is the name on the account?"

"Don't those glasses of yours remember my face?" Harry said.

"Sir, I need the name for verification purposes. We do it mainly to protect the children. You can never be too careful when it comes to safeguarding them."

"Oh... of course. It's Isaacson. Edward Isaacson."

Alex's eyes darted back and forth, a series of blinks navigating his access to the Isaacson family files. "Wow, I see. No problem. We'll get your children prepared immediately. Before I can do that, could you sign the required annual medical waiver for your family? Please note: We aren't responsible for the integrity of any data uploaded expressly at the customer's unique request."

Alex produced a paper-thin tablet from within his long coat, which Harry signed after a brief sigh of hesitation.

"All right, I'll take the kids to their classroom, where the technician is waiting. I'll return shortly."

"Wait a sec." Harry crouched down to address his children: "If they do or say anything you don't like, just yell for me, and I'll be right there. You hear me?"

"Yes, Daddy," Anna Lynn whispered.

"Yes, sir!" Braden shouted, a little too playfully for his father's liking.

With that, Alex escorted them to a room down the hall, where a young woman stood in the doorway. Her uniform matched Alex's, with the addition of a medical mask.

As Harry waited in the lobby, his eyes traced along the front desk and surrounding walls. The framed portraits of old donors were interspersed with students' artwork; the lack of recent additions denoted the tough times that had befallen the facility. Many of those who could afford to send their children to more modern, large-scale learning operations did so, even at the expense of their quality of life. Data transfer speeds and integrity levels had long illustrated the disparities between urban and rural, rich and poor. Now, as a public utility, data streams were subject to management—and mismanagement—by various local and state governments, each imposing its own designs for accessibility, efficiency, and content.

Meanwhile, nestled within private economic zones and firmly outside the grasp of these controls, the truly wealthy supplemented their children's digital lessons with hands-on learning, supported by a growing pool of otherwise unemployed professionals. Intelligence analysts, government staffers, financial consultants, and other white-collar workers made redundant by artificial intelligence could only hope to carve out a meager living in specialized education. A shrinking ruling class seeking to apply refined expertise to its methods of governance would have no issue in accessing such skills for the time being.

"So, your father was among the last true educators?" Alex's question rescued Harry from an internal spiral.

"What? How did you know that?"

"It's the information we have on file for the account. This says he was a teacher and a veteran—served during the Counter-Terror Era."

"Yeah, he didn't do much. Just pushed reports around or some shit. And a lot of good being a teacher did—educating poor city kids. He wouldn't let me join the service; said I needed college first. An engineering degree doesn't go as far as it used to."

Alex frowned. "I'm sorry to hear that. However, I'm glad you haven't let that stop you from supporting your children's education. Whatever they decide to do in the future, they'll be informed by the same foundation of knowledge that others their age will have access to."

"Braden's joining the Army as an infantryman as soon as he's ready. He's already told me that's what he wants to do. As for Anna Lynn... we'll see how things go as she gets older."

"Yes. Well, they're still both fairly young." A notification flashed on Alex's glasses. "It appears they have finished the procedure. I'll return with them shortly."

The kids stumbled back from their ordeal, a small bandage on each of their right arms. Harry wasn't looking forward to the ride home; it was a tossup whether they'd be agitated or pass out.

Harry kneeled and inspected them both. "Are you doing okay? How are you feeling?"

"They're going to be tired for a little while," Alex said. "It should wear off soon, though. Their brains are rather elastic. Far more so than you or I. Also, don't be surprised if their discussions today are a bit wild. They're just processing a lot of new data."

"Yeah... sure thing. Do you need anything else from me, or can I get them on home?"

"No, nothing else is required. You should have a receipt for today's services in your inbox. We've already charged the account on file."

"Hold on—" Harry navigated his personal device. "This shit gets more and more expensive every year! I bet those refugees from the 'Stans don't have to pay anything! Free healthcare, free education, free income! My dad didn't serve for this!" Harry's words erupted from the pit of his stomach. Anna Lynn stood motionless, her eyes and ears still more than capable of searing this moment into memory. Braden's face contorted into a self-righteous smirk, no doubt an imitation of his father that the boy associated with confidence.

"Mr. Isaacson," Alex said, "everyone pays the same for our services, regardless of whether they've escaped Central Asia's water conflicts."

"I don't give a single fuck!" Harry grabbed each of his kids by the wrists and dragged them out of the facility. Alex followed them with his eyes, his thick eyeglasses unable to halt the projection of his pity.

The first fifteen minutes of the ride back home were hushed. Harry reached for a stale energy drink and diverted his attention from the road to check on the kids. Their daze dissipating, Anna Lynn and Braden found their awareness while silently counting the autonomous semi-trucks moving in unison alongside them.

Braden's expression flashed wide with energy. "The word 'dinosaur' comes from the Greek words for 'great lizard.'"

"That's interesting," Anna Lynn said. "I learned that the Apollo 11 mission relied on four kilobytes of RAM. How is that possible?"

"It's not," Harry said. "There's no way any of that was real back then. And now they expect us to believe China has a base on Mars? What a joke."

Silence. On either side of the highway, rows of solar panels extended beyond the horizon. Long gone was the fragrance of citrus to bid travelers farewell as they transited the valley. Harry relapsed into a fantasy of righteous violence.

"The Taliban were adept at utilizing easily acquirable electronic components, such as solar panels."

Harry swatted Anna Lynn's words away, lost in fictitious renderings of his renown.

"I know. Did you see the SIGACT record where Pops went to the *madrasa*? They found a lot of bomb stuff there. He also helped those girls," Braden said.

"What did you say about Pops?" Harry's eyes bulged from an otherwise dormant mask.

Anna Lynn responded, her pitch veering into the robotic, "July twenty-third, two thousand eleven. Time: zero-three-hundred zulu. Sar Hawza District, Paktika Province, Afghanistan. Grid location: vicinity of four-two-sierra-whiskey-bravo-zero-seven-six-six. Task Force members investigate local madrasa suspected as IED cache site and were engaged by small arms fire. Compound cleared at zero-three-fifty zulu. Battle damage assessment: one servicemember wounded in action, five enemy killed in action, two civilian casualties, both female children."

Harry's grip twisted around the steering wheel. *What the hell did they do to you, Anna Lynn?*

"After that, Pops and his friends helped build a school for the kids in that town. He said they didn't even know how to read," Braden said.

"Pops told you this? What are you talking about, Braden? He died before you could walk."

"He told us in class. Pops was one of our teachers this year."

"I knew they were filling your heads with garbage!" Harry scanned for the nearest exit. "We're going back to have a word." He became preoccupied with the weight of his pistol, the way the grip scraped along his palm, the image of a front sight consuming his target.

"Pops said he wants to talk to you. He said he made a mistake," Anna Lynn said.

"The mistake is mine; I should have never brought you kids to that school! I'm going to make things right, though. They'll take their lies back—so you can be children again. A lobotomy would've been better than this shit." Harry's boot grew heavier on the gas.

As he parked at the facility, Harry barked an order at Anna Lynn and Braden: "Stay in the truck! I'll come get you when they're ready to fix this." He stuffed the Beretta into his jeans and dashed toward the main lobby.

Anna Lynn turned to Braden. "I think we should help."

Braden found solace in obedience, his focus trained on the back of the driver's seat.

"Braden, we need to help them with Daddy." Anna Lynn tugged her brother's shirt.

"...Okay."

Anna Lynn helped her brother climb out of the truck, its height above the ground rivaling their own.

Inside, their father was mid-torrent: "You thought I wouldn't find out that you've brainwashed my children? You know, if I were a different person, you might be dead already. I'll give you a chance to fix this. Delete it, overwrite it, I don't care!"

"Mr. Isaacson, we've uploaded the curriculum explicitly selected by the account owner. It is a collection of coursework and lessons produced during the late twenties using publicly available information."

"Well, no wonder my daughter is spouting this shit. We didn't take back control of education in this state until well after that!" Harry's focus narrowed further, his selective hearing priming a tripwire mine.

Alex was growing uncharacteristically impatient. "The foundation we've cultivated in the minds of Anna Lynn and Braden represents the most expansive and exhaustive datasets available in our nation's history. I don't wish to speak for your father, but I believe he chose coursework designed before the Great Data Fracture for a reason. Per the agreement you signed, we cannot attempt to alter information after it has been committed to the neural pathways. Not only is the practice unethical, but it has also been proven to increase the likelihood of dissociative disorders."

"There it is! 'Great Data Fracture,' my ass! I knew they filled this institution with radicals."

"Daddy," Anna Lynn whispered from behind her father. Braden was at her side, his stare pooling on the floor.

"Cleansing the filth of the internet was the best thing that ever happened to this country!"

"Daddy."

"We should have taken it a step further and started using you people for fuel—"

Anna Lynn burst as she found her words. "Daddy! Pops said he needs to talk to you!"

Harry's rage subsided at the sight of his children, only to regain its footing as his father was mentioned. "And what is this about my father giving them lessons? You're manipulating his image to get my kids to buy into your bullshit?"

Alex's eyes were scanning across the inner surface of his spectacles, a needful distraction spurred by a subconscious urgency to flee, to put a barrier between himself and the growing threat. "Mr. Isaacson… Harry—your father personally recorded several hundred hours of lessons for inclusion in the curriculum—to be introduced to both children once your eldest reached the equivalent of middle school." Alex paused, catching sight of a source of relief. "If you'll excuse me, your father left a document to be delivered to you at this point in their education. I apologize for not having noticed this sooner."

Alex's swift departure brought silence to the lobby, its pale white walls constricting and diffusing the emotional fever. Harry turned to Braden, the sudden change in atmosphere restraining his words. "I thought I told you to wait in the truck."

Anna Lynn answered for her brother: "I made him come with me. It really is Pops, though! He told us about Grandma, and when she went away, just like mom did."

"Hey, they're nothing alike," Harry said. "What your mother did to us is unforgivable."

Alex returned in a slightly disheveled state, an envelope in his hand. "This is for you."

"I seriously doubt—" Harry snatched the envelope from Alex. The paper was yellowed yet well preserved, his name written on the front in his father's characteristic all caps. The centering, the spacing, the envelope's seal—all perfect, just as Edward Isaacson would demand of himself… and of others. Harry's brow unfurrowed as he scanned the letter inside, the obsessive care with which each word was crafted authenticating the overly pensive man behind them.

I have failed you in more ways than one. I thought that continuing as an educator would make up for my past, for the pain and regrets that eventually drove your mother away. I did everything I could to shield you from my worst experiences, realizing too late that I deprived you of learning from them. Our country and the world appear to be experiencing challenges that far outpace any institution's ability to adapt. I fear that my parenting has failed to develop the generational resilience that will be necessary for an Isaacson to see the other side.

I began developing lessons for the grandkids not long after Anna Lynn was born. I could see what was happening to your marriage and knew they would need all the support I could provide. Economic troubles, a loss of career and purpose, the severing of relationships—these are enough to drive any man into isolation. They similarly have a long-established habit of guiding people into the arms of grifters, populists, and nihilists. They preach of a return to simpler times, to security and safety under the fundamentals of faith and tribe, and to answering the call of the void. The result is always the same: tattered banners and the complete inability of peoples to weather even the slightest hardship.

I spent over a decade supporting small communities of people as they struggled to drive out these influences and rebuild from the ground up. I did so with the understanding that my government maintained common goals, weaving resilience into organizations, infrastructure, and shared identities. I was clearly expecting too much. Failure after failure, I watched as ignorance, enabled by

*corruption, so easily swallowed up our efforts, our blood, and our
resources.*

*I would have liked to talk this through in person, to explain the
decisions I made in your childhood. Unfortunately, I must ask
you to settle for an archived version of me. I've produced a series of
lessons with the help of this facility, where we can interact further.
I hope to see you there, for the sake of your children.*

Harry sighed before crumpling the letter and flicking it at
Alex's chest. "This proves nothing. It's not him."

"I know it's him! You never listen to me!" Anna Lynn said,
her eyes watering.

"That's because you don't know anything. Those book
smarts are worthless, especially when they come from these
people. You know what? I'll prove that it's not your grandfather.
I'll go in there and confront whatever it is these radicals used on
you. After that's done, Alex here will either fix you both or be
forced to deal with me."

Harry unclenched his fists and pressed hard on his forehead.
If only he had served, perhaps things would be different—a job,
a purpose, and a means to battle his insecurities in a foreign
land. The kids' mother might still be in the picture. Or maybe
he would have met a different woman entirely, someone like
him, untainted by college or modern depravities. If, in fact, his
father was digitized and stored somewhere in this facility, Harry
intended to tell him about his plans for Braden. Ed Isaacson
wouldn't be creating another generational mistake.

Alex commanded Harry's attention, albeit with a slight shake
in his voice. "I'll escort you to the classroom, then. Your children
can wait in the lobby and I'll provide them with something to
keep busy."

"No, they're going to sit there and be quiet. There's no need for you to speak to them any longer." Harry motioned for the kids to sit and proceeded with Alex down the hall. A technician was waiting in the nearest empty room, motioning Harry toward the single reclining chair at its center.

This classroom was anything but. The seat was decrepit, the vinyl crumbling and adhering to the exposed skin on Harry's arms. On his right stood a rusted rolling tool tray and an IV fluid bag. On his left, a chain of desktop computers, daisy-chained together and buried underneath bundles of wires, struggled to continue whirring against a decade of dust and high temperatures. An external neural interface helmet rested precariously atop the pile of machinery. It was a relic from a time before manufacturers felt comfortable implementing planned obsolescence in neural interface systems, meaning it was perhaps still reliable.

This is where my money goes, huh? What a clown show!

The technician entered Harry's view while scanning over the Isaacson files displayed on their glasses. "Afternoon, Mr. Isaacson. How are we today?"

Harry gave a rigid nod.

"Good! Good. Let's get you hooked up for today's procedure."

Harry nodded again, this time only with his eyebrows. His gaze alternated between the technician's name tag and long, painted eyelashes. *Great, now I have to listen to this genderless freak.* The technician interpreted his expression as a sign of concern for the procedure.

"Not to worry," the technician continued. "We'll perform a standard course upload of the files available under your account. We'll begin by administering a general anesthetic, which will place you in a coma-like state. The neural helmet I'm preparing here will then flash these data files along your neural pathways. You'll experience the lessons as highly vivid memories. Keep in mind that time flows differently in this condition—something necessary for you to explore each lesson in a more deliberate manner. Otherwise, we'd be no different from your standard dream factory—heh. So, do you have any questions?"

"No, let's hurry this up; my kids are waiting."

"Oh... I'll wake you up within the hour."

Harry's thoughts strayed to Anna Lynn and Braden as the technician placed the neural interface on his head and connected the IV. As the drugs took hold, his vexations retreated from the technician's honed eyebrows and collapsed into the absence of self.

"Hello, son. Now that you're here, we can get started."

Harry recognized his father's home office, a spacious room made cramped by piles of old books, many of which were rare even before their banning. Their value starkly contrasted with the room's cheap furniture and shelving, their frames warping under the weight. Ed Isaacson sat hunched at his desk, oxygen mask in hand, with a determined look in his eyes that alone sustained his presence where his body was failing.

"Let's cut the crap. I know you're a fake," Harry said.

Ed's image shifted. He was now standing, his gaze focused on the point where Harry's form was concentrated. "Does that Rembrandt on the wall still give you nightmares? Is the one-eyed man still staring at *you*?"

Harry couldn't admit that the reproduction behind his father's desk had stolen his glances since he entered the room. The crowned subject of the painting, binding his conspirators with an oath, returned Harry's gaze. In his youth, Harry felt judged by the figure, its grim features communicating an expectation of who the boy would become. He sensed that judgment now, but for his failures to establish his worth as a man. It was not unlike the look on his father's face, which further anchored Harry to the memory construct.

"Now, I can't answer all your questions, as these are just recordings. However, I did my best to anticipate the conversations we could have, and there are many paths you can take during our discussions." Ed paused to allow a deep cough. "It's about time I tell you about my past. I've deprived you of the depth of my experiences, and it's only supported the development of your insecurities."

"My old man told me he never did anything useful in the Army. How could your experiences be of any use to me?" Harry said.

"Well, sometimes we lie to our children—the same way we lie to ourselves. I needed to hide my past from you out of fear that it would damage you and that you would see me differently." Ed's image glitched faintly, his oxygen mask present again, muffling his words. "The fact is that I was a tool serving our government's incessant need to conduct violence. I provided the refuge under which our incompetent leaders expanded their wealth and influence. It wasn't until my experience at the madrasa that my perspective began to shift."

"You had Anna Lynn talking about this shit. What the hell did you put in her head?"

Ed flashed away into a seated position, his eyes unfocused and yet glued to one of the few spaces on his desk not occupied with clutter. "We had reports of an IED maker operating out of a religious school, one of several along Afghanistan's lawless eastern border region used to indoctrinate rather than educate. The compound's only entrance was wired with explosives, so we breached through a wall. Our targets in the madrasa sent out a child wearing a suicide vest to meet us as we entered. We had no choice but to shoot her. They detonated the bomb by remote—luckily, we only received concussions from the blast. We eventually cleared the building, but another child was killed in the process. I still remember the looks on the faces of the little survivors as we brought them out, confused and angry, a coating of zealotry not yet set by age and experience."

Harry's vision widened, his diction reworking itself into the shape of a smile. "Shit, Dad, that's badass. Sounds just like the movies! Why didn't you tell me about this sooner?"

Ed was overcome by static and another prolonged cough. "The reason is simple: It's possibly the worst event I've experienced. Can you not see that?"

"Tell me another story about Afghanistan. Did you kill any more after that?"

Ed rippled with electronic noise. His clothes became disheveled, and the surrounding office now showed signs of neglect. Harry remembered this version of his father's frailty; the recording must've occurred shortly before he was committed to hospice care.

"You'll have to forgive me, son, if I don't show more emotion with this message. It's difficult talking to an empty room. If you've reached this point, it's apparent that I can't simply tell you what I've experienced. I can't break through whatever walls you've built, brick by brick, with ignorance, hate, and fear. I'll have to show you. I'll have to shock your system to the point that my words will have meaning again."

Ed and the classroom abruptly faded away, leaving Harry's consciousness in a void.

"Hey, what the hell is this?"

Ed's voice returned. "I engaged some fellow educators with experience in neural interface design to produce the closest thing possible to my sensory recollections. The facility you're currently lying in is unaware of this data and its potential consequences. What I'm about to do is highly dangerous, but I believe it's necessary for the sake of the Isaacson name. Either you will understand the true cost of your ignorance and course-correct, or I will introduce a batch of corrupted data files that will leave you in a permanently disabled state."

Harry's psyche trembled, his outburst wavering from his point of view as if held in a nightmare of impotence. "You're not taking my kids away from me! Goddammit, I knew you were after them! I'm getting out of this shit, and I'm taking Braden straight to the recruiter as soon as he's old enough! I won't make the same fucking mistakes as you, Old Man!"

"That's true," Ed's voice echoed from the darkness, "nor will any Isaacson repeat my mistakes."

Harry's being dissolved, leaving only flashes on the canvas of the senses.

The smell of dirt and human feces brought forth by chemical explosives. Through the haze, a child makes small steps approaching, green eyes cast upward, wounded. There's confusion and anguish. Muscle memory directs the fight-or-flight response. She's rocked backward by impacts. She falls still, and then, a cloud of dust and being.

A man lies on a paved road, the lower half of his face a red mass with vague remnants of teeth. Beside him rests a bicycle adorned with colorful tassels and a seat fashioned in the likeness of a teddy bear, speaking to the mental age of the former human. A voice: "Hey, come look at this retard!"

A woman's body is rolled out of a vehicle at a security checkpoint; illegible Pashto smears a sign hanging around the neck. Her arms are missing.

An Afghan man dressed in police attire stands above the remains of several men, either bent with age or yet unmarred by the sun. The neat lines of the surrounding fields are now stained with craters, robbed of their future harvest. The man kneels and places an AK-47 within reach of each body.

An emaciated father comes to terms with himself in the bathroom mirror. Blood and mucus spatter the sink. Lungs, inflated with trapped air, feel fit to burst through a distinct rib cage. Among the brain's simplest demands, long since obliterated with the scents of smoke and JP-8.

"Hello, is this Susan Isaacson? ... My name is Alex. I work for the César E. Chávez Rapid Education Facility. Yes, we have you on file here as next of kin for the children of Harry Isaacson. ... The children are fine. It's Harry. He's unresponsive. ... We need you to come to the facility as soon as possible. ... You're their aunt? We've called emergency services. Are you able to take them into your care while he's looked after?"

"Susan, thank you for coming." Alex was blanched, his pigmentation merging seamlessly with the surrounding near-sterile environment. "Can you speak with me in private?" he said, removing his glasses.

"Yeah... sure," Susan said as she walked past the two children in the lobby. Both appeared malnourished, a feature that was only further highlighted by their excessively tanned skin. Their shaggy, amateur haircuts hid their eyes, which were too tired to focus on the tablets Alex had provided.

"I shouldn't be telling you this, but I'm still trying to understand what happened to Harry... I've seen nothing like it. He seems to be awake. He just... isn't there. Our preliminary scans indicate that the customer-produced data we uploaded was corrupted, perhaps intentionally. Do you have any insight?"

Susan sighed, her eyes relaxing with realization. "My father was a tyrant in his own right, and his worship of progress seems to have followed him into death. Jesus, I can't believe he'd do something this drastic."

"You must understand how dangerous this is for the children. Experiencing a trauma such as this so shortly after the procedure, we don't know what will happen. Can you protect them from this?"

"I'll do my best. Fuck, I've got a lot to figure out."

"I will help with this conversation as much as I can. Shall we?"

"Yeah. I'm ready to meet them."

As Susan returned to the lobby, she paused to examine her relations from afar. Rightly suspecting that something was wrong, Anna Lynn had begun to dote on her brother, preparing him for whatever was coming. Braden was rigid in his seat, eyes forward, hands in his lap, and again wearing his father's face.

Contributor Log

I'd like to thank my *Kanenas*, my column of support, without whom none of this would have been possible. Thank you for being here to hold up the mirror, for your encouragement, and for your understanding. I love you.

S.P., you have a gift for recognizing the knots in my writing and providing the objective, academic lens required to combat my obsessive nature. You've known me since the beginning. Had I never committed to this path, the one that made this book necessary, I believe we would have conquered the world by now. Perhaps this is for the best.

Vladimir Chebakov, thank you for bringing my idea to life through your art. This book's cover serves as its first impression to the world, one that I am proud to present.

To *you*, the reader, thank you for making it this far. I wish you the best of luck on your journey as you navigate this world.

And to the woman who taught me to read and write, who sat with me at the kitchen table all those hours—my thanks are not enough.